Intoxicating

Also by Heather Heyford

The Crush

A Taste of Sake

A Taste of Sauvignon

A Taste of Merlot

A Taste of Chardonnay

Intoxicating

An Oregon Wine Country Romance

Heather Heyford

LYRICAL SHINE
Kensington Publishing Corp.
www.kensingtonbooks.com

To the extent that the image or images on the cover of this book depict a person or persons, such person or persons are merely models, and are not intended to portray any character or characters featured in the book.

LYRICAL SHINE BOOKS are published by

Kensington Publishing Corp.
119 West 40th Street
New York, NY 10018

Copyright © 2017 by Heather Heyford

All Kensington titles, imprints, and distributed lines are available at special quantity discounts for bulk purchases for sales promotion, premiums, fundraising, educational, or institutional use.

Special book excerpts or customized printings can also be created to fit specific needs. For details, write or phone the office of the Kensington Sales Manager: Kensington Publishing Corp., 119 West 40th Street, New York, NY 10018. Attn. Sales Department. Phone: 1-800-221-2647.

Lyrical Shine and Lyrical Shine logo Reg. U.S. Pat. & TM Off.

First Electronic Edition: March 2017
eISBN-13: 978-1-60183-826-1
eISBN-10: 1-60183-826-3

First Print Edition: March 2017
ISBN-13: 978-1-60183-827-8
ISBN-10: 1-60183-827-1

Printed in the United States of America

Chapter One

"Thanks for coming! Good seeing you again."

Poppy Springer scooped the coins left on the crumb-littered table into her pocket as she watched Sandy and Kyle Houser wheel their stroller out into the September afternoon.

Behind them, a stiff gust of wind sent the bell above the door clanging like a fire alarm. A page torn from a coloring book soared off the table and landed at Poppy's feet, only to skitter out of reach when she bent to pick it up.

Outside the café window, the couple didn't get far before Sandy paused the stroller to pull up the hood on her toddler's jacket.

Must be a storm brewing.

Poppy remembered the day that Kyle had balked at holding Sandy's hand in line at Clarkston Elementary. Now those two were expecting their second baby in May—though just this morning they had come to a mutual decision to wait a bit before telling anyone.

Poppy couldn't help but feel like the residents of Clarkston had become blind to her existence, discussing personal matters between bites of toast while she stood inches away, denying her the small courtesy of looking up when she topped off their coffees.

Poppy gave Sandy and Kyle the benefit of the doubt. They weren't rude, just preoccupied with their full lives. Besides, hadn't her father, known as Big Pop, always called her his human barometer—his teasing way of saying she was too sensitive to others' moods and emotions?

She slid the highchair out of the way, squatting to scrape up the congealing yolk of a dippy egg, and strode to the other side of the café to pick up the cartoon picture of a princess whose face was scribbled almost beyond recognition.

She was still gazing at it when the doorbell jangled again, and she looked up to see Heath Sinclair, Junie Hart, Keval Patel, and Dr. Red McDonald bluster in. The humble café her parents had named after her was the unofficial center of the tight-knit farming community, and Poppy had been a fixture there since birth. Along the way, she'd accumulated more friends than she could count, but she was particularly close with this diverse group, and her insides warmed like one of those rare autumn days when the sun filtered through the Oregon mist onto the vineyards and the pickers' carelessly discarded jackets were bright spots of color on the ground between the rows.

Ten minutes later, Poppy rested her tray on the table edge and began distributing drinks and sandwiches. She felt the strain in her back and arms more than usual today, thanks to a late night of studying. For Poppy, book learning had never come easy.

Heath snapped shut the large hardbound volume he'd been leafing through and shoved it in his backpack.

"Red, here's your spicy Italian wrap. Junie, sticky bun. Keval, are you sure all you want is spring water?"

Keval sighed. "I'm on a cleanse."

"Heath—turkey BLT and lemonade." Her eyes flickered to his, then back to the food she handed him.

Poppy had known Heath forever. But since she'd come back to work at the café, the air between them had somehow changed. Maybe Big Pop was right. Maybe she *was* oversensitive.

"Thanks," he murmured, cramming his backpack onto the seat behind him.

Poppy was much better at reading faces than pages, but anyone could see that Heath was hiding something.

"How do you do that?" asked Junie Hart as Poppy deposited the empty tray on an adjacent table. "Always remember everyone's order without writing it down?"

Poppy just smiled and slid into the vinyl booth next to Red, who often stopped by between patients at her counseling practice a few doors down.

"Poppy has a great memory," said Heath.

She flushed with pleasure. She was used to getting compliments on her looks, never her intellect. Heath wasn't a man of many words.

If he made the effort to say something nice, you could bet it was sincere.

She sought out Heath's hazel eyes to make clear her appreciation, for once not caring if it made him uncomfortable. *"Thank you,"* she said with emphasis.

But he was already intent on deciding on the best angle from which to attack his BLT.

At twenty-eight, Heath's angular face was still boyish. He had a naturally trim build beneath his fitted plaid shirt, and wavy hair the golden brown of the filberts that used to be ubiquitous to the Willamette Valley—until the Pinot boom came along and farmers uprooted the nut trees and replaced them with wine grapes.

Poppy folded her arms on the table and observed her companions as they ate and drank. Who would have believed that the brewery Heath had started in his basement would become so successful? And that Red, whose real name was Sophia, would one day be voted Clarkston's Best Therapist? Keval did I.T. for the local wine consortium, plus a few select clients on the side. Junie had taken the reins of her faltering family vineyard, and her work was paying off in increased sales.

All of them had made impressive strides over the past decade. All except Poppy. How did she even get to sit at the same table with the likes of them? With every step forward, she took two steps back.

She sighed. A few months ago, the little wine shop in Portland that she managed was sold, drying up her main source of income. She couldn't help but think that maybe the prediction written about her at graduation was destined to come true.

"I saw Big Pop at the vet this morning," said Keval. "He told me your news. Exciting!"

"What news?" asked Red.

Poppy hesitated. She hadn't decided how much to tell her friends about her long shot for the future, in case it didn't pan out.

At first when Cory Anthony—*the* Cory Anthony, one of Portland's top chefs—mentioned he might be able to put her knowledge of wine to good use at the new place he was opening up, she'd been ecstatic.

Then, during the formal interview, Chef told her the elaborate renovations were going to take longer than originally thought. The target opening date had been pushed back until the end of the year.

But the real clincher was that though he said he was impressed by Poppy having taught herself about wine, his job offer was contingent on her becoming official—earning her sommelier certificate. Her elation had given way to panic. She was a terrible test taker. To this day, she still had nightmares about school.

"First I have to pass that exam," she told her friends.

"You'll pass. You've got a great bedside manner," said Keval. "Besides, it doesn't hurt that you look like that classic painting of Venus on the half-shell."

"Thanks—I think." Another well-meaning comment equating her worth with her appearance. "And it's called table service. The parts of the test are wine theory, tasting, and table service."

"Excuse me," said Keval, waving his fork in the air. "Do I know all those fancy wine terms? Promise me one thing. Once you're a famous lady somm with your face plastered all over, you won't forget your roots."

She chuckled. "I can safely say that's not something you'll ever have to worry about."

"You've heard, right?" exclaimed Keval to the others. "Poppy's been, quote unquote, discovered by a talent scout who happened to be having dinner where she used to hostess part-time. Not only is she going to be a wine steward at Cory Anthony's latest place, she's been tagged to be the new face of Palette Cosmetics!"

"Easy," said Junie, dodging Keval's utensil. "Here, Keval, eat part of this sticky bun. I can't finish it. Poppy, what's he ranting about?"

But Keval couldn't seem to help himself in his frenzy to be the one to spill the beans. "Am I making this up? Her father told me himself. He was leaving the vet's office with Jackson, and Miss Sweetie and I were on our way in. Miss Sweetie adores Jackson. Anyhoo, between the fabulous new restaurant, the modeling, the private parties, and the jetting off to who knows where—well, I'm just saying. Take a good hard look at her. We might as well say good-bye right now to the Poppy we know and love."

Heath's face paled to the color of the milk in the small pitcher sitting between them.

I'm going to kill my father first, and then Keval, thought Poppy.

"But I was just getting used to having you back," Junie pouted.

She and Junie had been spending more time together since Manolo, the itinerant engineer who'd created Junie's tasting room during last fall's crush, disappeared as mysteriously as he'd arrived.

"We've all missed her," said Keval hurriedly. "But what kind of friends would we be if we stood in the way of what she really wants?" Red chimed in. "Details, please?" Keval started to say more, but Red cut him off. "From Poppy, if you don't mind."

Poppy clenched her hands in her lap, her excitement tinged with nerves. "Well, it's far from a sure thing. The Palette people liked my test shots, but they're waiting to see if I pass the test and get the wine steward position. Everything hinges on that. So, I guess we'll just have to wait and see."

"It's a thing now for companies to use a so-called real person with an authentic career in their ads instead of a full-time model," added Keval, stuffing the wad of cinnamon-encrusted dough Junie had given him into his mouth. "What's hotter than a lady somm?" he asked around his mouthful. "Everybody either wants one or wants to be one."

Keval had a way of putting a dramatic spin on things, yet he was right about one thing. The day would come when a somm was a somm. But for now, flaunting women sommeliers was a way for restaurants to get buzz.

Red squealed and hugged Poppy as best she could in the narrow space between the table and the booth. "That's fabulous!"

"Go Poppy!" said Junie from her seat by the window, raising her mug in a salute.

All these premature congratulations made Poppy anxious. She looped her ponytail around her hand again and again until she noticed the right angles poking against the canvas of Heath's backpack. She pounced on the chance to change the subject.

"What's that?" she asked playfully, craning her neck.

"What?" replied Heath.

"That book."

"Nothing. Just a book." He drained his lemonade and wiped his mouth with his napkin.

"Our old high school yearbook," said Red.

Poppy's smile dissolved. "That's ancient history." She had long since thrown her copy in the Dumpster out in the alley behind the café. But not before the senior superlative that yearbook editor Demi

Barnes had managed to sneak by the advisor had become fixed in her mind.

After all these years, it still hurt.

Anyone else would have been content to stick with the traditional lines: Best Dressed, Most Likely to Become President, and so forth. Not Demi. She'd had it in for Poppy since seventh grade, when she found out Daryl Decaprio, the guy she had a crush on, was playing Poppy sappy love songs over the phone at night.

In a small town, your senior superlative defined you like an epitaph carved in stone. Except unlike an epitaph, you weren't dead when you got it—you had to live with it for the rest of your life. Demi had used her creative writing skills to create the ultimate parting gibe.

"What made you haul that out of storage now?"

Junie said, "You know Heath. He doesn't like letting go of things."

Heath gave Junie a look, causing her to blush, while Keval fidgeted with his spoon.

"You were saying?" prompted Red, smoothing over Junie's gaffe.

Cautiously, Junie continued. "Our tenth class reunion's coming up. Didn't you get the invitation?"

"I haven't checked email for the past couple days," said Poppy. Lately she'd been spending every free minute studying.

"Well, anyway, Heath and I thought it'd be fun to look at faces. You know, jog our memories. Guess who'll show and who won't."

Heath pulled out his phone, tapped something in, and handed it to Poppy. "Here. Read this."

Instantly, Poppy stiffened. Heath knew her trademark fault better than anyone. How could he put her on the spot like this? Surely everyone around the table could see the signs of rising panic: her shallow breathing, the pink climbing up her neck to her cheeks. She had trouble with the simplest things. Texting. Making grocery lists. Reading instructions. People said, "practice." What they didn't get was, even a word she had read a hundred times could look different the next time.

She swallowed and slid her damp palms down her thighs. *You're not stupid*, she told herself firmly. But her shame at being dyslexic was still paralyzing sometimes, especially when she had to read out loud, in public. And not being able to control her shame made her feel guilty. Inadequacy, shame, guilt—a vicious cycle.

Heath held her gaze. "Go ahead," he said evenly. "You've got this."

She felt his strength seep into her. Haltingly, she reached for the phone and bowed her head over the screen. The letters of the alphabet swam and shifted before coalescing into a pattern of rune-like shapes.

"Deep breath," said Red gently.

Dutifully, she inhaled and attempted to decipher the words. "Clarkston High School Ten-Year Reunion," she read haltingly. "The Radish Rose. Dinner and dancing. RSVP to Demi Barnes, Reunion Committee Chairman."

"First Saturday in December. So, who's in?" asked Red, clasping her hands atop the table.

"I am," sang Keval with a wave of his fingers.

Of course Keval would go to the reunion. Reunions were made for people like him. Following four years of exceptionally awkward adolescence, Keval was a walking "it gets better" ad.

"It'll be good for business," said Junie. "I don't get out enough as it is, what with running both the vineyard and the winery."

Red looked at Poppy. "What about you?"

"Think I'll pass." She handed Heath's phone back and attempted to bolt, but Red stopped her with a hand on her forearm.

"Aw, come on. It'll be fun! Dancing, seeing people you haven't seen in forever . . ."

"That's after Poppy's test. She might be living in some Portland penthouse overlooking the river by then," said Keval.

Maybe not a penthouse. But she'd better have some place in her sights. If not, that would mean she had flunked the test, failed to get the sommelier position, and was doomed to keep living at home with her parents. And also that Demi had been right about her all along.

"She can come back for it," said Red. "It's only an hour's drive."

That might be true, but learning two new, high-powered jobs and all that went with that was going to require all Poppy's time and energy. It wouldn't be like before, when she could hop in her Mini Coupé and run back to Clarkston on a whim. That made this endeavor all the more nerve-racking—finally leaving her friends and parents behind to really strike out on her own.

Still perched on the edge of the booth, Poppy ventured to ask Heath, "Are you going?"

He shrugged. "Don't know."

Heath had come a long way since his own senior superlative: Most Likely to Blow Something Up. He'd been on the watch list of the Clarkston F.D. since sixth grade, when his attempt to build a geyser with a pack of Mentos, a liter of soda, and duct tape worked a little too well.

Poppy smiled to herself, forgetting her own problems for a moment. Heath had always been somewhat of an enigma. Their teachers used to murmur behind their hands that he was a science prodigy. Who could forget his Edible Skin Layers Cake made from Fruit Roll-Ups (epidermis), Jell-O (dermis), and mini marshmallows (hypodermis)? Rumor was, he'd aced his college boards. Yet he'd tossed out all those scholarship letters without opening them, and now beer drinkers all over the Pacific Northwest couldn't get enough of his ales with names like Newberg Neutral and Ribbon Ridge Red.

When it came to social skills, there was a sweet innocence about Heath that made him hard to get close to.

Given Heath's case of arrested development, Junie didn't waste her breath pressuring him. Everyone knew he'd rather face an angry rattlesnake than make chitchat at a party. Instead she focused on Poppy. "Don't you want to see all the people we went to school with?"

"I've never stopped seeing most of them," replied Poppy. Even during the four years she worked in Portland, she still lived at home. "For everyone else, there's Facebook."

"A lot has happened over the last decade. Some people went away, some got married, had kids, got divorced, won and lost jobs..." mused Red. "People change."

"Exactly. That part of my life is behind me. I don't feel the need to see how I'm measuring up."

"But how can it hurt?" pleaded Keval. "Come on, Poppykins. It won't be any fun without you."

She set her jaw. Finally, she said to Heath, "Hand me that yearbook."

Outside, rain pelted the windows, and there was the rumble of distant thunder.

Poppy thumbed through the pages until she found what she was looking for. She laid the open book in the middle of the table and pressed her index finger to the passage that still haunted her.

Red, Junie, and Keval tipped their heads and read silently, while Heath's eyes skittered restlessly around the room like he'd rather be anywhere else but there.

Most likely to still be a Clarkston waitress at our tenth class reunion: Poppy Springer. Poppy's most endearing talent is writing her name backward. She is a true golden retriever at heart, as evidenced by her blond mane and a mind refreshingly free of deep thoughts. Poppy's hobbies are organizing individually wrapped tea bags and leaving a trail of smiling faces wherever she goes.

Following a brief pause, everyone started talking at once.

"Are you serious?"

"Who cares about an old senior superlative?"

"That doesn't define you."

"Who's going to remember that? It was the freaking Stone Age."

Lightning flashed. The café door opened and a tall woman in a silk blouse and pencil skirt blew in, shaking the rain off her umbrella.

Demi Barnes had started out as an assistant at the statehouse down in Salem and worked her way up the ladder. Recently she'd nabbed the job of running their state senator's newly opened Willamette Valley satellite office—quite the achievement.

She paused inside the entrance, combing her fingers through her windblown hair.

Poppy was the only server working until the dinner shift came in at three. It was her job to greet Demi. Yet somehow, she found that her butt was glued to her seat.

When Demi spotted Poppy she started toward her, heels clicking ominously with every step.

From the corner of her eye Poppy saw Heath slam the yearbook shut and slip it into his bag.

"Well, look who." Demi stared down at the splashy orange flower on Poppy's uniform. "Back working at your parents' café?"

"For now," she replied. The crack in her voice betrayed the scars from Demi's subtle yet razor-sharp bullying, back when they were in school.

"Things didn't work out in Portland?"

Why does Demi always make me feel so inferior? It was her own fault for letting Demi get to her. Inadequacy, shame, guilt.

Somehow, she managed to mask her inner turmoil. "Things worked out fine. I'm just . . . back home temporarily, until my new job starts."

"Oh, really? What job is that?"

There was a roaring in Poppy's ears, and before she knew it she was back in second grade reading circle at Clarkston Elementary and Demi was laughing at Poppy's stab at reading about Danny O'Dare, the dancin' bear. To this day, though blessed in many ways, on some level she still felt like everyone was always waiting for her to mess up yet again. She looked around the table to see five sets of eyes on her, reflecting every emotion from encouragement to empathy to—in Demi's case—disdain.

Defiance welled up in her. She was tired of being talked down to. Underestimated.

She squared her shoulders and lifted her chin. "I'm going to be a sommelier at Cory Anthony's new restaurant."

Her heart pounded. *What am I saying?*

Demi's jaw dropped. She was speechless.

And Poppy was loving it!

Keval caught Poppy's momentum. A haughty grin spread across his face. "*And* a model. *Boom.*" He punctuated the syllable with his fork.

Demi's eyes swung back to Poppy's, seeking clarification.

"You've heard of Palette Cosmetics?" Poppy tossed her ponytail and stared straight into Demi's treacherous green depths.

I'm already in way over my head. Might as well go all the way.

"They've hired me to be their spokesperson."

What alien being has taken over my body?

As swiftly as Demi had been caught off guard, she recovered. "Isn't that special? You'll definitely have to come to the big class reunion, then! I'm sure everyone will be fascinated when they find out we have a sommelier *and* model in our class. In fact, spreading the word ahead of time might get more people to come."

The faces around the table froze.

Demi sensed weakness like a shark smelled blood. "That is . . . unless it's not a done deal?"

Keval said, "Oh, it's a done deal. Done as a dog's dinner. Tell anyone you want. Tell the world! Poppy Springer has evolved. Our golden retriever's going to compete at Westminster. Instead of sorting tea bags, she'll be sorting French chardonnay. In place of smiley faces, she'll be the face of—"

"Poppy's going to be a great somm." Compared with Keval's rising hysteria, Heath's voice sounded rock solid.

Poppy wanted to kiss him—even if it did make him squirm.

Red took advantage of the uncomfortable lull to start gathering up her belongings. "Nice to see you, Demi. Poppy, could I scoot out and pay? My next client's coming at two."

"I should get going, too," said Junie, reaching for her own bag.

Poppy let Junie out and remembered that for the time being, her job was pouring nothing stronger than Stumptown's Hairbender. She offered Demi a nearby table.

"Actually, I'm not as hungry as I thought," Demi said. "I've got an idea. We were going to have our reunion meetings at the Radish Rose, but I think this would be a better spot. The next one's scheduled for Tuesday evening. I'm going to go contact the committee. I'm sure they'll all want to hear all the details about your new job."

"I'll look forward to it," said Poppy, her smile feeling as phony as a three-dollar bill.

"Oh, and Heath? I just thought of something else. Get your dad to loan us some potted trees from his nursery. The theme this year is Bacchanalia, and some greenery will be just the thing for that Roman garden look I'm going for. Now, I've got some calls to make."

They watched Demi walk briskly out the door and down the sidewalk, umbrella in one hand, phone in the other.

Poppy's heart sank. If only she had kept her mouth shut! There had never been any expectations of her. She could have gone on working at her parents' café forever, and no one would have thought the less of her.

But now, if her fabulous new life didn't happen, she was going to be the laughingstock of Clarkston.

Chapter Two

"Ow," hissed Keval, rubbing his shin.

"I barely tapped you," replied Heath.

"Next time, try using your words."

"Next time, try not saying every word that comes into your head."

"Can you believe Demi Barnes walked in here just when we were reading Poppy's yearbook superlative?"

"After what she wrote, she's got nerve setting foot in here at all," muttered Heath.

"Nerve is something Demi has in spades. Did you hear her? 'Heath, get your dad to loan us some potted trees,'" Keval mocked. "How'd she ever get that job in Senator Hollin's office, with that kind of diplomacy? That's what I'd like to know." He shuddered. "What are we going to do?"

"Do?"

"About Poppy. You know how she is. She'll never pass a written test without some major academic intervention."

Secretly, Heath hadn't exactly been devastated when he found out Poppy had lost her job at the wine shop. Not that he didn't want her to be happy, but the idea of having her back at the café on a regular basis warmed him inside. No one else made his turkey BLT quite like she did: bacon fried crisp, light on the mayo. He had already started getting excited at the idea of her being present at all the town's big annual events—the post–Memorial Day Hike, the Clarkston Splash in July, and the fall crush celebrations, just like back in the good old days—when Keval broke the news of her plans to leave again in three short months.

He looked up from where he'd been staring into his empty glass. "A waitress at rest tends to stay at rest unless an external force is applied to her. Newton's First Law of Motion."

"That is so nerd."

"Nerd has such a negative connotation. I prefer intellectual badass."

Keval rolled his eyes and glanced over at where Poppy waited on another table. He inclined his head toward Heath's. "You know what I mean."

Heath did know. If not for that hotshot restaurateur who had set his sights on his Poppy, right now the world would be falling back into apple-pie order. But he couldn't exactly share that with Keval. Or with anyone, for that matter.

"Don't make me say it," Keval whispered.

"Say what?" Heath was lost in his fantasy of seeing Poppy's friendly countenance every day again, instead of only glimpses now and then. Not that he couldn't have found her if he'd needed to over the past few years. Her parents' house was right down the road from his. At least there'd been that.

"I love Poppy to pieces. Who doesn't? But let's be real. The eel-whay's inning-spay, but the amster-hay's ead-day."

"Pig Latin. Brilliant. Shoulda been a spy, like Sam."

Keval's eyes grew round. "Is it true what they say? Was Sam really a spy?"

Heath slapped his forehead. "And you think *Poppy* has a short attention span?"

Right before Sam Owens started the consortium, he'd been awarded a chest full of medals for his military service. When asked about the details, he was infuriatingly closemouthed. His reticence had turned speculation about his past into one of the town's favorite ongoing pastimes.

"Why are you asking me?"

Keval sat back and folded his arms. "Heath Sinclair, that is a hedge if I ever heard one. You're one of Sam's best friends. I knew it. I always said—"

"Forget Sam. Back to Poppy. You're right about her."

"Then you admit it—she's in way over her head."

"No." Heath instinctively rushed to Poppy's defense. Fate had first thrown them together when they were barely tall enough for the carnival rides at the Yamhill County Fair. Over time, they'd grown as thick as the tangled roots on one of his dad's overgrown perennials, and just as hard to separate. He knew her limitations better than anybody.

On the other hand, he couldn't deny that Keval had a point. "Maybe. Poppy might not be well-read, but she's not dumb. What I meant was, I agree she's going to need help."

He stopped short of volunteering himself. The truth was, he didn't want Poppy to pass that test. He wanted her to stay right there in Clarkston.

Keval, on the other hand, was plenty smart, but he didn't have the patience to spend hours tutoring Poppy. Heath felt safe bouncing the ball back to him. He gave Keval a penetrating look.

Keval glanced over his shoulder. "Are you looking at me?"

"Why not? Aren't you the cybermayor of Clarkston?"

"Just because I do promo for a wine consortium doesn't mean I know diddly-squat about wine. You were the one who held her hand all through school. With all due respect, if not for you, Poppy still wouldn't have graduated. And now you're in the beverage business. You're a shoo-in."

"I'm a brewer, not a winemaker." Heath's highly tuned olfactory senses worked as well for wine as for beer. But Keval didn't have to know that.

"Shhh—here she comes."

Poppy approached sporting her usual winning smile despite the incident with Demi minutes earlier.

Heath braced himself for her unique blend of orange blossom, jasmine, and sandalwood—a blend that never failed to stimulate a rush of cortisol and adrenaline in his blood.

"Anything else, guys? More water? Lemonade?"

"Aren't you upset?" Keval blurted. "I can't believe you just told Cruella de Clarkston that you already got the sommelier and the modeling jobs. What are you going to do if you don't pass your test?"

So much for zipping it, thought Heath. "No one would know anything about this if you had so much as an atom of self-control."

Keval's mouth crinkled into a suitably sheepish expression. "The news was bound to come out sooner or later."

Heath sighed and scrubbed a hand over his face.

"I'll think of something," Poppy replied. Her smile remained steadfast though her eyes sparkled wetly. Then her lips quivered as she gulped unshed tears. "Somehow."

Chapter Three

"Hey, boss."

Heath's marketing manager, John, stuck his head in Heath's office on his way back from lunch.

"I'm free to fill you in on yesterday's Brewer's Guild meeting whenever you are."

Heath looked up from the spreadsheet he'd been studying, rocked back in his chair, and locked his fingers behind his head. "How'd it go?"

"Same as last month. It was all about brewpubs again. That's all anyone wanted to talk about."

Heath sighed. "Sounds like a song on repeat."

For months, John had been trying to convince Heath to open a bar in the front of the brewery where they could serve their own brands on tap. And he wasn't the only one. Sam Owens had been hammering him, too.

Across from Heath's desk, John perched on the arm of a chair. "Think of the bucks we're missing out on. We can charge more per pint in our own bar than we can sell it at through our distributor. Not only that, in case you didn't notice, you're becoming a one-man cult. Your customers want to meet the brewer. They want to know *you*."

"*We're* becoming a cult," Heath corrected him, scooting his chair back in. "We, not me. I didn't build this business by myself. And I didn't start out brewing beer for the notoriety. I like to keep a low profile."

He bowed his head over his spreadsheet again, signaling the conversation was over.

John pressed his lips together. "Ironically, the fact that you've always flown under the radar has made you in even bigger demand.

Like it or not, you've become a recognized brand. We should have a point of destination where people can sample everything on the line."

"We're doing fine without a bar," said Heath, without looking up.

"We could do even better. When's the last time you went on a good pub crawl?"

In the early years of setting up his business, Heath had been in countless ale houses. But these days, Clarkston Craft Ales's phenomenal rise had him spending more time crunching numbers and plotting the next big idea with his brew team.

"What say you drive over to the city with me for the next guild meeting. We can spend the afternoon checking out the competition."

"That's what I got you for."

Wearily, John got up and turned to leave, but lingered in the doorway. Heath looked up. "That it?"

John gave the wall a resigned slap. "That's it."

When the sound of John's steps faded away, Heath sat back and scratched his head.

Both John and Sam had excellent business sense, and they weren't the only ones raving about brewpubs. He might not travel much, but he kept his subscriptions to the industry journals up to date.

But the thought of his own bar—schmoozing and posing for strangers' selfies—made him wince. His comfort zone was right here, behind the scenes.

Besides, what with checking on his dad every day, he had a full plate.

John was right about one thing, though. It wouldn't hurt to drag himself out of his lair and take a trip up to the PDX soon. It was long overdue.

A warm front had swept in on the heels of yesterday's storm, leaving the autumn air feeling almost balmy.

Fifteen feet up, in the wide-reaching arms of an oak, Heath flipped on the string of white lights hanging along the roofline of the tree house he'd started hammering together when he was eight years old, after his world fell apart.

He stood back, imagining how this place would look today through Poppy's eyes.

When Keval wussed out at the café, there had been nothing else to do but step up to the plate. No way could he resist those tears that Poppy tried to hide.

Still, this wasn't going to be easy.

He ran some water into a plastic cup with the name of one of his best-selling ales emblazoned on the side and watered the ivy hanging from a macramé cord.

Heath didn't deal well with change. Not even good change. The success of his brewery operation had been completely unexpected. He had never set out to be named one of the most successful craft brewers under thirty in the Pacific Northwest. At least once a week, someone asked him what he was still doing in tiny Clarkston, why he didn't move to the city. It was a logical question. Portland was the home of more breweries than any other city on earth. The consensus was that he ought to take his rightful place.

But Heath didn't want to move to Portland. He didn't want to move anywhere. All he wanted to do was experiment with his kettles and hydrometers and quietly run his business.

Anyway, to his way of thinking, being the only beer producer in a wine town was an advantage, not a handicap.

First thing he'd done when he could afford it was put away enough for Dad to live on when he finally retired from his tree nursery.

Next, he started building himself a *real* house on the land he'd been trespassing on since he was a kid.

The thought of Poppy coming up here tonight weirded him out. He'd had a few guys here, back in the days of skinned knees and hide-and-seek. But it had been a long, long time since anyone other than himself had stepped across the threshold.

But what else could he do? Poppy needed help. And they had an unspoken arrangement that stretched back years.

A fat yellow feline twined through his legs. She'd been a starving kitten when Heath first heard pathetic cries coming from the weeds along the edge of the Albertson's parking lot in McMinnville on a sweltering July day. After unloading the week's worth of food for him and his dad that he'd been carrying into his car, he'd gone back to investigate and found two terrified gray eyes staring up at him through the grate of a storm drain. He'd endured her wailing for two hours until someone from the county public works with the right tools finally came out and took the grate off. The loss of the meat and ice cream sitting in his hot car all that time had been worth it.

He named the kitten Vienna, after a trip he'd taken to learn about Austrian beer. That's where he saw an orphanage with a revolving crib built into its wall. Back in medieval times, when an abandoned baby was placed in the outside half of the crib and a bell rang, the monks inside would go retrieve it.

That's also what had given him the idea to cut a garage-sized hole in the wall of his tree house so that he could roll his double bed in and out, as weather permitted.

It was already October. There wouldn't be many more nights as warm as this one. It'd be a shame to stay inside. He rolled the bed out onto the porch then stood back looking at it, frowning. The tree house wasn't designed with company in mind.

Why was he obsessing? It was only Poppy.

The purple comforter looked wrinkled. He whipped it off, shook it a few times, and spread it carefully back on the bed.

There. That looked better.

Heath bent to stroke Vienna's soft fur, and she shut her eyes, bowed her head, and purred her appreciation. "That's all this is tonight, Vienna. A mercy mission."

He could still remember the first time Poppy had come to his rescue. Sam Owens's seventh birthday party. Heath's dad had to promise him yet another trip to the Museum of Science and Industry just to get him in the car. Even then, he'd sat with his arms folded tightly across his chest the whole way over to Sam's house.

Once Dad pulled away from the curb, Heath hid behind the sycamore tree in Sam's front yard, stealing an occasional peek toward the jungle gym where all the other kids clamored and shouted.

Outside, Guinness and Amber started barking, shaking Heath out of his reverie.

"Heath?" called Poppy, her voice carrying up from the wooded path, bringing him fully back to the present.

He held back the beaded curtain and peered down to see his pit bull mutts blocking the path. Beyond the dogs, in a swirl of fallen leaves, stood a vision in a jeans jacket over a long white dress. A slouchy patchwork bag was slung over her shoulder. The setting sun filtered through her skirt, outlining the shape of her legs, triggering an inappropriate tug of desire he pretended not to notice.

"Amber. Guinness. Come."

Tongues lolling happily, the dogs turned tail and galloped up the steep ramp Heath had built for them, first Amber and then Guinness on his three good legs. Both looked like completely different animals from the trembling, sad-eyed mutts Heath had found cowering at the shelter.

Poppy nodded toward the glass-and-steel structure up on the hill that was partially visible through the trees, now that the leaves had started to fall. "How's the new place? Did you move in yet?"

"Couple months ago."

"How's your dad doing since you moved out?"

For the past nineteen years, it had been just Heath and his dad in the old house, a stone's throw away. It looked exactly the same today as when Mom left. Heath had offered to take him shopping to buy some new things, but Dad wasn't interested in making any changes. Heath felt guilty leaving, but he was tired of living in a shrine. Besides, a man needed his own place.

"Helps that I'm right next door."

"I'll bet." Her candy-pink lips widened into a complicit grin. "Remember that time Old Man Waters chased us out of here?"

"Summer between tenth and eleventh." How could he forget? He had snitched four beers from the fridge, lodging two among the rocks in the creek to keep them cold. He and Poppy were sitting on a felled log dangling bare toes in the water, feeling very grown-up holding their beers when Mr. Waters had come stumbling down the bank with a raised fist, yelling for them to get off his property. They had hightailed it out of there in a hurry, sloshing beer in their wake, laughing so hard they doubled over, panting with relief by the time they reached Heath's property and safety. Was it their fault the finest swimming hole on the creek happened to be on private property?

Since then, Heath had bought out Waters for a fair price and had his ramshackle old house bulldozed. Now this entire hillside belonged to him.

Poppy stood at the base of the tree, looking around at the rope hammocks slung between branches, the fire ring Heath had built from fieldstone, and the brightly colored Adirondack chairs. "It looks way different than it did back then."

"I've fixed it up over the years. Guess you could call it a hobby. Come on up."

She climbed the boards nailed to the tree and emerged through the curtain, sending a thousand beads clacking.

He sniffed the air for her intoxicating scent. Tonight, the citrus topnote was diluted by the breeze, leaving him wanting more.

Poppy took a step in the direction of the opening in the wall and peered out toward the green Chehalem. "Is the rope we used to swing on still down there?"

"Still there. Been, what—twenty years? Don't know if I'd trust it. Probably pretty deteriorated."

Poppy's leg nudged the bed, inadvertently causing it to roll an inch.

"It's on wheels!"

"Casters." He demonstrated by rolling it back and forth a little. "I made it mobile, so you can fall asleep looking at the stars." No sooner had the words left his mouth than his face grew hot with their implied meaning. "Not *you*—"

Poppy smiled softly and turned her attention to the tree house's interior.

That was one of the things that made Poppy so great. She pretended not to notice when he stuck his foot in his mouth, which he tended to do every other sentence.

"If it looks like rain, I roll the bed inside and close the shutters."

"You've got a little galley kitchen and everything."

Heath pushed a button on a remote and the small screen hung high in a corner flickered on. He turned that off, pushed another switch, and music filled the tree house.

"Sweet," breathed Poppy, nodding with appreciation as she continued to look around.

Heath kept his expression neutral, but deep inside, he glowed at her approval.

Amber loped back down the ramp. Poppy bent to pet Guinness, curled up on the rug. "This would be a great place for a party!"

"You know how I am at parties."

Their eyes met, recalling as one the day when she had noticed him standing alone under that sycamore tree at Sam's birthday party, taken him by the hand, and led him over to where the others played.

Even in second grade, Poppy had never had to think twice about what to do, what to say, or how to act around people. It was her gift, just like Heath was driven to understand how things like temperature and pressure and the other forces of nature acted on matter, the stuff of the universe.

"This is my getaway. It's where I go when things get crazy."

She nodded in understanding.

Even when they were kids, she had accepted without judging that he was better one-on-one than in big groups.

"Look," she said, backtracking toward the curtain, sidestepping Guinness's bulk, "I appreciate you asking me here. But you're really busy, what with building a new house and running your business. We don't have to do this . . ."

"If I didn't want to, I wouldn't have offered."

"Are you sure?"

He lowered himself onto the bed and swatted the mattress. "Sit down. Show me what you got. I mean, your stuff. Er, you know what I mean."

Her childlike enthusiasm returning, she hopped up across from him, crossed her long legs in front of her, and pulled some folders from her bag.

"First, here's the multiple-choice exam I already passed."

Heath's eyes zoomed in on her grade, circled in red.

"Sixty-six?" he exclaimed, the words slipping out before he could catch them. "What's passing?"

"Sixty. I didn't say I aced it, I said I passed."

Barely.

"Okay. What's next?"

"Sitting for my Certified Sommelier Exam, the test I need to get my new job. If I don't take it within three years of passing the first one, I have to start all over."

"It all sounds very professional."

"It's pretty intense."

"But didn't you say the restaurant's opening in three months?"

"Now you get why I'm so stressed. Here, look."

He read aloud from the page she gave him. "'Part One. Table Service. Recommend, select, prepare, and serve wine in the appropriate glassware with skill and diplomacy.'"

"Diplomacy? You've got that nailed." Poppy was at ease around with types of people.

She shrugged. "I've been waiting on customers my whole life.

But I need more practice popping champagne corks without putting someone's eye out and pouring the bottle evenly on my first trip around the table. The biggest assortment of wines in town is at the consortium. I told Sam I'd foot the bill if he agreed to proctor some mock tastings. Will you be one of my pretend customers?'"

That sounded simple enough. "Tell me what to do."

"I'll recruit enough people to fill up the table and hand out information about all the wines ahead of time. All you have to do is act like finicky diners. Challenge me to figure out which wine you want by asking probing questions, and I'll try to guess what it is and serve it."

"Could probably get Holly and Junie to come. They know a lot about wine."

"Great idea. So, we're good on table service. Keep reading."

"'Part Two, Practical Tasting. Identify six different wines, tasted blind.' How are you on that?"

"It's a matter of naming three whites and three reds in twenty-five minutes. I just need someone to pick and pour the wines so that I can't see the labels, and then I'll try to determine what they are."

"I've done that. It's the same as tasting ales."

"Then comes Part Three, the part I'm nervous about. I have to write about the classic regions, grapes, and terms."

This was where things got tricky, thought Heath. "You must have learned a lot working in the wine shop or you wouldn't have started down this road."

"I memorized pictures and terms from studying labels. Having visuals to go with the words really helps. But there was no pressure. I could take my time. And I didn't have to write anything."

Heath recalled a game they used to play in Mr. Lu's class. One student left the room. Another hid. Then the first student came back and had to guess who had hidden.

"You always killed in that Who's Missing game."

"Training myself to be good at memorization was the only way I managed to get through school. But you know that."

Heath did know. He'd tutored her on and off for years in exchange for her smoothing the way for him at school and parties. If not for her, his social life would have been as empty as his home life.

He leafed through the rest of the folder. "You'd think they would come up with a way for people to take the wine steward test orally."

"This isn't public school. The governing body for sommeliers might allow that, eventually. But I don't have time to wait. It's on me to adapt, or else it's back to the café. Back to square one."

" 'Part Three, Theory, examines comprehensive knowledge of wines and wine production. Candidates are given one hour to complete a written exam.' "

"Here's a sample question," said Poppy, pulling a paper from the sheaf. " 'Define and compare the following viticulture practices: sustainable, organic, and biodynamic.' " Lowering the paper, he frowned. Poppy knew her limitations, otherwise she wouldn't be here, asking for help. Still, he was a realist. "Writing aside, can you talk about this stuff?"

She chuckled. "All day long. It's reading the questions and writing the answers in the time allotted that gives me a problem."

"Obviously you're going to memorize the sample questions. What do you want me to do?"

"I'll dig up material that I think will be on the test. You make up questions based on that and quiz me orally. I'm not nervous around you. I'll be able to take my time coming up with answers. I'll write everything down as I go and then read back over it on my own until I have it down cold."

More than once, Heath had seen Poppy break down in tears over the most basic written assignment. He skimmed over the rest of the questions with growing doubt. This exam was no walk in the park, even for someone without dyslexia. He could feel her eyes on him, waiting for a response.

"Well? What do you think?" she pressed, looking worried.

"I don't know . . ."

He felt the mattress shift as she sat back, discouraged. "You think I've bitten off more than I can chew."

Now was his golden opportunity. Without realizing it, Poppy had just dangled the key to his future within his grasp. All he had to do was reach out and take it.

She couldn't pass this test without his help. If he refused, she wouldn't be going anywhere. He'd have her right there where he wanted her. Thanks to all they'd been through together, she trusted him implicitly. Whatever came out of his mouth next she would do, without question.

He'd be a fool to throw this chance away.

Tasting victory, he plunged ahead before his conscience could intervene. "Look . . . you're right. This is a bad time. Building the house has already taken me away from the creative side of the brewery for too long. I need to catch up. Plus, I've got development targets, marketing goals . . ." He pushed back the lock of hair that was always falling into his eyes, tempering his rejection with a wry grin. "Can't even find time for a haircut."

"I understand," she said with a quiet resignation that nearly ripped a hole in his heart.

She began gathering her scattered papers into a pile as he tried to quell the rising panic inside him.

No. He couldn't do this. She had just arrived at his tree house, and now she was leaving. He had to drag this out until he came up with a better solution.

"What's wrong with Clarkston?" he asked, provoking an argument. Anything to make her stay.

She stopped what she was doing. "Nothing's wrong, it's just that I need to move on."

"Why? Because of some dumb thing someone put in the yearbook?"

She turned on him, red-faced. "It's not just 'some dumb thing'! It's me. Or what people think of me, anyway. 'Stupid Poppy.' "

Exasperated, she began cramming her messy pile into her bag.

"Have you thought about looking for another hostess job or a wine steward position that'll take you on the basis of the test you already passed?"

She shook her head as she yanked her overstuffed bag, papers peeking out of it, onto her shoulder. "That's okay. I'll figure it out."

"If it's just about being in Portland, you could find work as a server tomorrow, even without your certification."

She avoided meeting his eyes. "I'd be working at least forty hours per week, with no prospects for advancement. I'm better off working thirty at the café, studying in my off hours, and saving money by living at home. Besides—" She stooped to retrieve a paper that had slipped onto the plank floor.

"What?"

"I promised Red I'd model in her fashion show."

Something in her tone caught his attention.

"Fashion show?"

Cautiously, her eyes met his. "It's a benefit. You know, for people going through hard times. And people who are sick."

They shared a look full of meaning. Heath knew all about hard times . . . serious illness.

She hiked up the strap on her bag that was slipping down her arm. "There was no reason to bring it up before. No sense in dredging up bad memories."

Hayden. He'd died years ago. But it hadn't ended there. The death of his twin had shattered the family to pieces. When no one else could—or would—look out for Heath, the Springers had stepped up to the plate without a second thought. And now Poppy was *still* protecting him.

And here he was, making her believe she was incapable of reaching her dream so that he wouldn't have to face her leaving. Who was the *real* loser?

"Anyway, I promised. Figured it'd make me feel useful while I'm stuck here, studying for my exam."

She unfolded her fawnlike legs and set one foot on the floor.

"Wait."

She stopped in the midst of hoisting her body off the bed and looked up at him.

"I'll coach you."

"Really?" Slowly, she sank back down.

If she failed, he would have himself to blame. That only added to the cost. But if life had doled him out his share of tragedy, it had also given him broad shoulders. And the hope in her eyes was worth missing a few meetings. Even having to face a life without her, if that's what it took to make her happy.

"It would mean so much to me, Heath."

"I'm not gonna lie. It's going to be tough."

Poppy threw her arms around him, catching him off guard.

Behind her, his hands hovered inches over her back while his preganglionic sympathetic nerves released acetylcholine, speeding up his heart rate, stirring stagnant blood, and tightening his muscles in the textbook "fight or flight" response.

"Stay and love" had never been one of the options.

Tentatively, his palms came down on her silky hair. Her sweet, tart scent filled his senses . . . her body was warm and lithe, pressed up against his.

It wasn't the raw, sensual attraction itself that terrified him. He might be a klutz at cocktail parties, but he didn't need the lights on to find his way around the bedroom.

It was that these were *Poppy's* arms gripping him in a stranglehold . . . little Poppy, who had talked his ear off after school at her parents' café until his dad got home from work.

Poppy, whose incessant chatter at the science club meetings his dad insisted they invite her to in return made everyone lose track of their experiments.

She pulled back until her hands rested on his shoulders.

"How soon can you do a mock tasting?"

It took him a second to remember what they were there for.

"What about that reunion meeting next week? You told Demi you already got the job. How are you going to fix that?"

Poppy's hands slid into her lap, leaving him feeling relieved and at the same time, robbed of something priceless.

"I got a little carried away there, didn't I?" She laughed drily. "I figure the best thing to do is dial it back a bit—admit to Demi the fact that I have to take a little test as a requirement for the new job. I don't have to add that I happen to be scared out of my mind about it."

"Watch out. Demi Barnes is a ballbuster."

But Poppy was already on her feet, her usual, sunny grin restored. "Thankfully, most people aren't like Demi. I'm hoping there'll be some friendly faces on the reunion committee."

Heath wasn't nearly as optimistic as she was. But then, who was? "Just saying. Be careful, and don't let anything Demi says bother you. You're smarter than you think."

She put one foot below the other as she climbed down the ladder with the burden of her satchel. Despite her disability, she was so bold, so brave.

"Careful," he called, wishing he could wrap her in a cocoon of protection wherever she went.

Watching her shoes stir up the new-fallen leaves as she made her way back up the path, his heart squeezed. Poppy had always been there for him. He would do whatever he could to help her pass this test, even if it meant losing the best friend he'd ever had.

Chapter Four

The following Tuesday Poppy arrived for her three o'clock shift with a bounce in her step. She had a plan, and people willing to help her implement it.

For most of her life, Poppy's world had revolved around the comfortable two-story home and the café her parents had named for her. Her mom had a smile for everyone, and her dad's cheerful personality was contagious. Everyone told her she'd gotten the best of both of parents.

On the wall above the register, framed photos marked the pivotal events of her life.

The first, grainy baby picture showed her slouched in one of those infant bouncy chairs, perched on the counter only inches from where she now stood. In the next, she was taking her first wobbly steps, holding on to a chair seat. Then she was about eight, one of her mom's aprons knotted behind her neck, her tongue out in concentration as she carried a brimming water glass in each hand while helping out during the busy crush season. She could still remember how proud she'd been when she hadn't spilled a drop.

When she was thirteen, she begged to be allowed to wait on customers. After she proved she could heft a tray full of heavy restaurant china used for its home-style cooking, there'd been no holding her back.

The final picture depicted all five foot seven inches of her in her pale blue prom gown bought special in Portland at the new Macy's that had swallowed up Meier & Frank, the Bon Marché, and Marshall Field's. The photo was snapped at the moment her hand caught the crown that kept slipping off her sleek blond head, as if it didn't quite fit.

The day after prom, Poppy tossed the crown into an old shoe box, but Mom had that snapshot framed and hung at the end of the row. Now there was no room on that wall for more pictures. It was as if being prom queen was the pinnacle of Poppy's success.

By the time she graduated, no job at the café was beyond her. She could greet customers with a smile as welcoming as Mom's and close out the register at night as good as Big Pop, and even pinch-hit at the grill on the days when the cook didn't show.

After a while, Poppy forgot about that last picture of herself. She'd become a grown-up. She figured she'd learned all she'd ever need to know.

It wasn't until her former classmates began trickling back to town, flush with accomplishments and talk of exotic-sounding places they'd seen and interesting people they'd met, that Poppy started to feel vaguely uneasy every time she caught a glimpse of that photo's fading colors. Did being crowned prom queen really represent the high point in her life? Was it all downhill from here?

She began to get the sneaking suspicion that she was missing out on something. What that something was, she didn't know. But she thought it was high time she found out what the world held outside of sleepy Clarkston.

She took the first job she was offered: stocking wine at a dusty shop tucked into a Portland side street. Portland was an hour's commute on a good day, longer during the fall crush when the two-lane roads were packed with thirsty wine-country tourists.

Within three years, she had memorized the shop's entire inventory. Then one day the manager quit. Poppy was happily surprised when absentee owner Saul Rankow phone-promoted her, though she had moments of self-doubt when she suspected Saul just didn't feel like leaving sunny Arizona in the middle of the winter to look for a more qualified candidate.

That promotion was no meaningless honor for someone having been born with looks that fit some stereotypical image of beauty. She was determined to show Saul that he hadn't made a mistake. For a year, she ran the shop single-handedly. Her knowledge of wine impressed a certain customer, who offered her a hostess job at his restaurant on weekends.

That led to more connections. Soon, she was poached by a more upscale establishment where she got to see firsthand what a wine steward did. He told her someone with a memory like hers could make a career in wine if she got her sommelier certificate.

It took her another year to get up the guts to take the two-day introductory course.

Passing that test was her second big milestone.

Still, she stayed at the wine shop and took the odd hostessing job on weekends.

Then one day, Saul flew up from Arizona, his skin baked to the distressed texture of an old leather couch. He had come to tell Poppy in person that the business had been sold and the shop was being torn down to make way for a bank.

It was back to square one.

It'd be one thing if she had never left Clarkston. But leaving and coming back in the wake of losing her job—even through no fault of her own—made her feel as if she had failed.

If anything could give her back her self-respect, the sommelier and modeling jobs could. She had three months to make them happen.

Poppy wondered again who else to expect along with Demi for the meeting. She was on good terms with practically everyone in town, so she wasn't particularly worried, despite what Heath had said.

C-a-y-e-n-n-e. L-e-m-o-n-s. Poppy stuck out her tongue in concentration as she penned a shopping list of perishables when just before seven, a threesome came into view outside in the twilight.

Demi entered first, dressed in the latest style.

Following were Demi's high school best friend Jess Hoffer and . . . *Keval?*

Poppy sat them down and distributed menus. "Something to drink?"

Demi skimmed the front and back of the laminated plastic and thrust it back at her. "I'll have a Mexican mocha."

"Me too," said Jess, aping Demi, just like old times.

Poppy frowned. "Sorry. We're out of cayenne. I just put it on my list of things to pick up at the store."

With a sigh of disgust, Demi sank her chin into her left palm and dismissed Poppy with a wave of her right. "Just give me a black coffee, then."

"Me too," said Jess.

"I'll have water," said Keval. "My cl—"

"Your cleanse," Poppy said for him.

The women ordered food and chatted while they ate. Immersed in her duties, Poppy picked up a word here and there concerning the band, the menu . . . typical reunion plans. Keval sipped his water, uncharacteristically quiet.

Poppy relaxed a bit more. It seemed as though Demi was never even going to bring up Poppy's aspirations. Maybe all her worrying had been for nothing.

Before she totaled their check, she went over to ask if they wanted anything else.

"Why don't you have a seat?" asked Demi, patting the vinyl beside her, as if Poppy were indeed her retriever.

She looked around the room, hoping to see someone flagging her for more catsup or a drink refill, but all of her other patrons seemed content for the moment. She had no excuse not to lower herself next to Demi.

"So, I was thinking that we should set up an event page with all the reunion information such as the place, date, ticket registration, and fun throwback photos. And who better to do that than Keval? He blogs for a living."

That explained Keval's presence.

"Well, it's more than blogging . . ." Keval started to say, but Demi horned in before he could finish.

"Also, I'd like to reach out to our classmates with some pre-reunion teasers. Posting pictures and videos can direct traffic to our event page. When people link back to us on their own social media sites, it'll really help create buzz. I thought we could include a bit about you and your new position, Poppy. Wouldn't that be fun?"

Poppy squirmed. "Er, I guess. To be clear, I still have to take a qualifying test."

"What do you mean, a test?"

"It's just a formality, but I wanted to mention it."

Sniffing controversy, Demi's eyes lit up. "What does that entail?"

"Confirmation that I'm qualified to be a sommelier. Like I said, it's just a formality." Talking about it dredged up the excitement just below the surface, and she couldn't help sharing more information than she'd intended. "Sam Owens is letting me use the Clarkston wine consortium to have a mock service and blind tastings." No harm in mentioning that.

"I have a great idea! Keval, you should go to the mock service and report on Poppy's progress."

Keval opened his mouth, but nothing came out.

"It's not very interesting," Poppy hastened to add. "A few friends pretending to be difficult customers, to prepare me for any service eventuality."

But Poppy could see Demi's wheels turning.

"When's the first one?"

"When?" Poppy was a poor liar. "Sunday afternoon around four, about an hour before the consortium closes. It's not very busy at that time of day. But—"

"Sunday. Take note, Keval. I'm counting on you to deliver. People are going to eat this up."

"But—"

"Actually, I might come, too. Four, did you say?"

Before Poppy could answer, Keval said, "The consortium will be open. Just show up."

Poppy shot him dagger eyes.

Keval shrugged. "Just trying to be helpful," he said sheepishly, to no one in particular.

"Good! I'll see you both, then. Are we finished here? I have mountains of work to do when I get home," Demi said, not waiting to hear anyone else's point of view. She turned off her tablet and slid it into her bag. "We'll take our check now."

"Yeah. We'll take our check," said Jess.

Keval hung around the café after the other two women left.

"What the . . ." Poppy's hands went up in the air.

"Sorry. The way you talked the other day, I didn't even think you cared about the reunion."

"That has nothing to do with you reporting on my every move between now and December!"

"It's not every move. It's just a few little wine tastings."

"A few little—?" she sputtered. "You know how much this means to me. My stomach's already tied up in knots!"

"But this will be perfect! Don't you see? I can skew your story any way I like. You know: Yesterday's valedictorian is today's meth addict. Former quarterback's now a balding Uber driver. The beloved teacher who wrote your college recommendation barely remembers you . . ."

That last one seemed to hit home. He frowned, momentarily lost in his thoughts.

"What I see is you, covering your ass."

"Maybe I am. But I'm right."

"And how do you propose to skew *me*?"

Keval tapped his upper lip with his pointer finger and thought. "'Small-town barista becomes high-class wineau'?"

"*That* doesn't make me sound like an alkie."

"How about, 'Café namesake aspires to loftier lodgings'?"

Resolutely, Poppy folded her arms. "And you call yourself a blogger?"

"Let me work on it. Something along the lines of 'we are all masters of our own destiny' or 'our lives are what we make of them.'"

"Wait until Heath hears that you and Demi are going to be at the mock service. I'll be lucky if he shows up."

"Don't tell him."

"Are you telling me to lie?"

"I just said don't tell him. Unless you want to scare him away."

Poppy dropped onto the seat across from Keval. This simple practice session that she'd promised Heath was going to be among close friends was turning into a zoo.

Chapter Five

On the day of the mock service, Poppy picked up Heath and drove him to the consortium.

"Lot of cars here for an hour before closing," said Heath suspiciously.

"Well, Junie promised to come . . ."

"That accounts for one car. What about the other dozen?"

"Maybe there's some consortium business going on."

"This late on a Sunday afternoon?"

"We'll find out soon enough."

Inside, Sam had draped a round table in white linen and set six places. Around it sat Holly Davis, the consortium's wine rep; Rory Stillman, whose family were cider makers; Junie; Keval . . . and Demi Barnes.

Poppy stopped in her tracks.

Heath peered over her shoulder at the table. "Did you ask Demi to be part of this?"

"She said she might come. But I was hoping she only intended to watch. I didn't think she was going to actually participate," she replied, the knot of tension growing in her stomach. She watched the six chatting as if they hadn't a care in the world, suddenly wishing she were sitting among them instead of about to perform. What had she gotten herself into? In twelve years of school, she had barely passed from one grade into the next. She was sure a couple of teachers only passed her because she made an effort to be extra pleasant and helpful. But the sommelier test was a whole other world. Who was she to think she could suddenly do something so ambitious?

All the consortium's two- and four-tops were filled, and Poppy recognized some wine growers, a cellar master, and a distributor standing around, talking over their wine. A few of them waved to Poppy, and she waved back nervously.

The atmosphere crackled with expectation. Nothing like this had ever happened here before.

"There she is, the woman of the hour," said Sam.

"I thought you said this was a slow time of day?" Poppy muttered under her breath.

"Apparently word of your mock tasting got around."

"Who . . . ?"

"Don't look at me. But I'm not surprised. Sommeliers are having a moment. Anyone would be interested in getting a glimpse of what you have to do to become one. Especially the people around here, in the middle of Pinot country."

Sam rested his hand on Poppy's back. "You feel as stiff as a board. Relax! This is going to be fun. Heath, that empty chair is yours."

Heath went over and took his place.

Without his reassuring presence next to her, Poppy gulped.

"We're all ready for you," said Sam. "I snapped a photo of the instructions for Demi and Keval, and they've been going over them, thinking of questions to stump you with. How you feeling, champ?"

He gave her back a brisk rub to go with his pep talk.

"I was feeling fine, but now . . . Sam, I was only expecting to wait on four people, not six. And I thought there might be a few people milling around, but I wasn't counting on being the center of attention—putting on a show."

"Aw, you'll do fine. The harder it is now, the more it'll help you in the long run, right? Isn't the whole point of this exercise to help you perform under pressure?"

"Yeah, but . . ."

"Look, I apologize. I didn't know there'd be this much fuss, either, but what can I do? Kick everybody out? You want my advice, just ignore the rubberneckers."

She whooshed out a breath. "Easy for you to say."

"Do you want me to just tell everyone there's been a change of plans? I can do that."

That wouldn't be an auspicious way to start out. "No."

He checked his watch. "Your choice. I'm not rushing you, but it's five after. I imagine your friends have other things they could be doing."

The door swung open, heralding four more people.

"I'll be right back," said Sam.

Poppy used the opportunity to center herself.

When he returned, she sucked in a breath. "Let's do this," she said on an exhale.

Sam smiled. "You'll do great."

He escorted her over to the table. "Can I have everyone's attention?"

The room quieted.

"If you just happened to stumble in on this fine autumn afternoon hoping to sample some Willamette Valley wines, you're in for a double treat. You locals already know my good friend, Poppy Springer, from her parents' café on Main Street. What you may not know is that Poppy is preparing to take her sommelier exam. We're happy to support her by doing a mock table service. Now, for those who aren't familiar, becoming a certified sommelier is a daunting process. An important part of it is demonstrating excellent serving skills. Poppy's pretend customers here are going to pepper her with questions to see how well she can answer them. I've set out an assortment of wines ahead of time that they can choose from. Poppy will have to guess what they want from their hints and then pour it according to highest industry standards."

He looked around the table, rubbing his hands together. "Are we ready?"

"Ready," they responded.

The spectators jockeyed for the best viewing positions.

Poppy smiled nervously.

"We're awfully thirsty over here," said Demi.

"Let's get started, then," said Sam brightly. He raised his glass to Poppy. "Good luck."

"Good luck!" came a chorus of voices from around the room.

Poppy approached the table. "How is everyone tonight? I'm Poppy, and I'll be happy to take your order. Who would like to start?"

To Poppy's surprise, Keval trained his phone camera on her and proceeded to video her.

That wasn't part of the plan.

"What are you doing?" she asked, breaking character.

"Don't pay any attention to me. Just keep doing your thing," said Keval without lowering the phone.

She would deal with Keval later.

"I'll start," said Holly.

Poppy decided her best option was to ignore Keval. If she was going to be a model, she'd better get used to being on camera.

"What are you thinking this evening? Anything on our menu catch your eye?"

"I'm hungry for a juicy steak. What would go best with that?"

"You can't go wrong with a pinot noir for its earthy truffle notes."

"Sounds good!"

Maybe this won't be so terrible.

She moved clockwise around the table to Rory. "And you, sir?"

"I'm vacationing here in Pinot country, but I prefer white wine to red. What can you recommend?"

"Do you like a soft, buttery wine or a crisp, green apple flavor?"

Those who knew Rory broke out in knowing smiles. Around these parts, the name Stillman was synonymous with cider.

"Definitely apple."

"I'd try one of our excellent Rieslings. They're aged in steel tanks instead of oak barrels, which gives them a bright edge that'll make your mouth water like a tart Granny Smith."

Rory laughed. "Sold."

She moved to Junie. "Ma'am?"

"Today is my birthday. I want to order a couple bottles of champagne for the table."

Junie's birthday was in April. She was just doing her job, trying to think up a way to stymie Poppy.

"First, happy birthday! What a great way to celebrate, with champagne. To clarify, only wines made in France using what's called the champagne method can technically be called that. I'll be happy to show you one. Or we have a lovely sparkling white wine from California that's a great value."

"The California will be fine. Can you get that for us now, before you finish taking everyone else's order?"

Poppy glanced at Holly. "If it's all right with you?" Technically, since Holly had established herself as the host, she called the shots.

Holly nodded. "It's fine. But could you upgrade that sparkling wine to champagne?"

"No, no," Junie protested.

"I insist," said Holly. "My treat. And could you get that right now? We really are thirsty."

"Absolutely."

Poppy set six champagne flutes on a service tray and carried it to the table, distributing a glass before each diner. Now came the tricky part. A bottle of champagne had as much air pressure as a car tire. The room went silent. Most of the spectators were in some aspect of the wine business. They knew as well as she did that more people were killed each year by flying corks than by horses, falling icicles, or football injuries.

Poppy's palms were damp and slippery. Carefully, she held the serviette over the top of the bottle as she loosed the wire cage around the neck. One slip, and she could see the headline on Keval's blog: "Wine Tasting Takes Deadly Turn as Inept Sommelier Takes Out Innocent Bystander."

A manslaughter charge could significantly lower her odds of passing her test if the judges got wind of it.

A stray hair escaped from her ponytail, tickling her forehead. She held her breath and twisted the bottle.

The cork came out with a gentle hiss. She poured a little into a glass and held the bottle with the label showing while Holly took the first sip.

After Holly nodded her approval, Poppy circled the table clockwise, filling first the ladies' glasses. One, two, three . . . she counted the seconds to be sure she was pouring them to the same level on the first try. Then she went on to pour the gentlemen's in the same way.

Flawless, if I say so myself. From the corner of her eye she noted nods of approval from the peanut gallery.

After the table had toasted and downed their glasses, it was Demi's turn to order. So far, she had been on her best behavior. Poppy remembered Red saying that people had changed over the past decade. Maybe Demi had changed, too. Poppy was always inclined to give people the benefit of the doubt. And with the way things were going so far today, she was gaining confidence, as well.

She approached Demi's right side. "And for you?"

Demi drained the last drop in her glass. "I'm loving this champagne," she said, smacking her lips. "How about another round?"

This really was turning out to be a piece of cake, thought Poppy as she retrieved another bottle.

Once again, the cork came out without injuring anyone and the first glass was approved.

But no sooner had Poppy poured the round when Demi said, "It's a beautiful fall day. What do you say we take this party outside?"

No one seemed to know how to respond. Leaving the designated setting wasn't part of the script.

"I'll take that as a yes." She looked at Poppy and, with a smile that would melt butter, said, "We'll take our drinks outside, at the picnic table. You go first; we'll follow."

"Certainly."

Poppy got the tray and went around the table again, aware of all eyes intently fastened on her as she painstakingly collected the brim-full glasses, hoping no one noticed how she trembled.

When the tray was filled, she carried it in her left hand toward the door and let herself out, the glasses tinkling like wind chimes.

Outside, she dispersed the glasses around the picnic table and waited with her bar towel over her forearm for the diners to arrive.

And waited.

After what seemed like forever, Sam poked his head out. "Come on back in. Demi changed her mind." Then he lowered his voice and with a conspiratorial smile added, "Once a bitch, always a bitch."

Sam remained in the open doorway to hold the door for her once she'd collected the champagne flutes yet again.

She shook her head. "I appreciate it, but no one will be holding any doors for me during my exam."

Sam shrugged. "Your call."

Again, she managed both the tray and the door. As she crossed the room to the sound of sleigh bells, her face was on fire.

Demi had made a fool out of her in front of all these people.

Still, she'd survived. What could happen now?

As she reached the table, her rubber sole caught on something, pinning her foot behind her while momentum kept the rest of her moving forward. At the end of Poppy's arm, the tray teetered as she tried to save the pricey champagne at risk of hurting herself, but too late.

The world started spinning in slow motion, heightening her awareness of details around her. The blue plaid shirt of the cellar master. The fold marks on the unironed tablecloth. The horror on Junie and Holly's faces, and the triumph on Demi Barnes's.

A wave of champagne preceded the forward motion of Poppy's body.

Throughout the room, hands flew to mouths. There were gasps, followed by the sound of shattering crystal.

Poppy's foot came out of her shoe at the same time her hands and knees hit the floor.

The metal tray banged against the back of Demi's chair, clattered to the ground, and rolled across the floor until it hit someone's ankle. There it spun like a top for what seemed like forever, finally coming to rest with a metallic clatter.

Keval caught the whole thing on video.

Heath's arm shot to Keval's hand and pushed his phone to the table. "Turn that thing off."

He was the first one to reach Poppy, followed closely by Sam. Heath lifted her up from behind, one hand supporting her elbow, the other curved around her rib cage beneath her breast.

"Ohhhh!" Demi shot to her feet and shook her arms, flinging sticky-sweet droplets across the table onto Junie and Keval and the others. "She got me *soaked*!" Her cries drowned out Poppy's yip of pain when her bare heel went down on something exquisitely sharp.

Heath guided Poppy to his chair next to Demi's and immediately knelt and cradled her foot in his lap. "Let me see."

He snatched his napkin from the table and held it to her heel.

As Poppy bent to see red bleeding into the white linen, Heath reached up, and with his fingertips to her breastbone, pressed her into her chair back. "Don't look."

First day of summer vacation after fifth grade. A broken Coke bottle, half-buried in the mud on the bank of Chehalem Creek. Ever since then, Poppy couldn't stand the sight of blood.

But too late.

Her stomach roiled. Her strength seemed to seep out with her blood until her head swayed backward in a most humiliating manner.

Hands cradled her head, and she opened her eyes to see Sam's concerned face, inches from hers.

"You'll be all right."

Then Sam and everything around him began fading into oblivion.

Her hearing was the last to go. From far away she heard Sam say, "That's it, folks. Thanks for coming . . ."

Chapter Six

Poppy rested her bandaged foot on the dashboard while Heath drove her car from the primary care clinic in McMinnville back to her parents' house.

"*That* went well," she said in a voice dripping with sarcasm.

"Does it hurt?" asked Heath.

"Just my pride." She pulled her phone out of her bag. "I've got to catch Keval before he posts that video. You'd think he'd have enough sense not to without being told, but then again, it is Keval. You know how he loves drama . . ."

"Too late," said Heath.

Poppy's hand froze. "What do you mean?"

"That was real-time video he was shooting."

"Real-time? As in, live?"

"On the new social media site set up for the reunion. With an automatic notification to every one of his connections."

"Oh no!" Her hand with her phone in it dropped to her lap. "Think of how many contacts Keval must have!"

"And every one of them can share with *their* contacts."

Painstakingly, Poppy typed *Clarkston Class Reunion* into her phone.

"Aaarrgh!" she moaned after she watched the horror movie starring herself. Her head fell back against her seat.

"It's not that bad."

"Not that bad? This has almost a hundred views! Wait—"

Her hand flew to her mouth. "Oh no."

"What?"

"Cory Anthony saw it."

"How is that possible?"

As soon as the words were out of his mouth, Poppy and Heath looked at each other and said simultaneously: "Demi Barnes."

"I'm fried. I'll never be able to walk down Main Street again. I might as well quit."

"You fell. People fall."

"I didn't just fall. I fell reaching for my life's goal—which happens to be public knowledge, now that I was stupid enough to tell Demi Barnes about it!"

Heath's frown made Poppy immediately regret complaining. Heath could withstand a great deal of pain, but he couldn't bear to see another creature struggle. His menagerie of scruffy pets was testament to that.

She threw her hands in the air. "Okay. I won't quit. But from now on all my practice sessions are going to be private."

"No. You can't do that," said Heath.

"You want me to subject myself to public humiliation again?"

"You have no choice. You have to avenge yourself. Show Cory Anthony and everyone else that you have it in you to fight for what you want."

"But what if I don't have what it takes? Service was supposed to be the thing I'm best at, and I totally screwed it up! What if I bomb in the actual test?"

"You won't."

"How do you know?"

"You have to think like a proton."

Poppy scowled. "A proton?"

"You know. Positive."

"Talk English to me."

"Protons have a positive charge, versus electrons, which are neg—"

"You're making my head explode."

"You've got to get Keval to post a new video, this time of you doing something well. Replace the bad impression in peoples' minds with a good one."

"I can see me now, limping around the table, waiting on diners."

"Give it a couple of weeks. Work on the other parts of the test while your foot heals."

"Invite Keval to film me doing a blind tasting?"

"What could go wrong—as long as you're seated this time?"

* * *

Heath held the door while Poppy used her crutches to hobble into the house.

"Poppy!" exclaimed her mom. "Are you okay? I've been trying to call you the past couple of hours! Why didn't you pick up?"

"I take it you saw."

"Of course I saw. I'm Facebook friends with Keval."

My own mother.

"Sorry. I had my phone turned off turned for the tasting."

"Here, sit down on the couch. What did the doctor say? Was there much blood?" Mom glanced at Heath, standing in the doorway with his hands shoved into his pockets. "She doesn't like blood. Ever since that day she stepped on that broken Coke bottle—"

"You okay, then?" Heath asked Poppy, one foot pivoted toward the exit.

"Oh, sure. You don't have to stay. Thanks for taking me to the clinic."

"Do you want me to run you home, Heath?" asked her mom.

"I'm good."

Heath's new house wasn't so close that you could see it from Poppy's, but it was an easy walk. Over the years, they'd each done it hundreds of times.

"Thank you for taking care of our girl," said Mom. "But don't rush off. Don't you want to come in? Joe's out jogging." She went to the window and peered anxiously up and down the road. "I worry about him every time he goes out, that he'll get hit by a car or have a heart attack or something." She turned back to Heath. "I brought home stickies from the café. They're yesterday's, but they're still good."

Heath slid one hand from his pocket to wave awkwardly. "No thanks. I got some stuff to do to get ready for the workweek."

"Sunday evenings always go by so fast, don't they? It'll be Monday morning before we know it." She looked at Poppy's foot and it dawned on her. "How are you going to work tomorrow? You'll have to take some time off."

"I'll manage."

"You can't wait tables on crutches."

Mom meant well. But when would she start treating Poppy like a grown woman who could make her own decisions?

Heath stuck his head back in the door and said, "The doctor said she's to stay off it for at least a week."

Poppy stuck her tongue out at him. "Tattletale."

Some grown woman I am.

"A week!" aped Mom. "Well, we'll manage for a week. Maybe our part-timer will want some extra hours. Heath, are you sure you don't want a sticky? Wait—I'll wrap some up for you and your dad."

Mom disappeared around the corner.

"When can you get together to practice a blind tasting?" Poppy asked Heath as they listened to the crinkling of plastic wrap from the kitchen.

"I'll get the key to the consortium from Sam. We can do it after hours. I didn't mean 'do it.' I meant sneak in. To do the tasting. You know. Alone. Without anyone watching."

Poppy hid her amusement.

"Don't worry. I know what you mean."

Mom gave Heath his buns and watched him start to walk down Chehalem Creek Road. "Such a sweet boy. And after all he's been through."

The Springers and Sinclairs were friends even before Mom offered to let Heath hang out with Poppy after school every spring and fall during their elementary school years while Heath's dad labored at his tree nursery.

"You think you know someone," she mused for what must've been the hundredth time. "After all these years, it's still hard to fathom Diane walking out on Heath and Scott."

"At least his brewery is doing great."

Mom turned away from the storm door and walked over to the couch, her frown melting into a soft smile. "You always did look on the bright side. That's one of the things that makes you special."

"If anyone deserves happiness, it's Heath."

"Scott hardly ever comes in to the café anymore. Sometimes I think he's turning into a hermit." Mom sat down next to her. "Now, tell me what the doctor said about that foot."

"It's nothing, really. I'm to keep taking my antibiotic so it doesn't get infected."

"Well, thank goodness you're here, where I can take care of you, instead of off in Portland living by yourself."

Poppy sighed. *Here we go.* Another mom rant about Poppy wanting to leave and get her own place.

"Now don't roll your eyes at me. You have a good life here. Lots of friends and a family who loves you. A nice home, with plenty of room."

"I know, Mom. We've been over this."

"It used to be enough."

It was—until she noticed everyone else moving forward while she was stuck inside the café, looking out.

"And now you're talking about moving into some tiny apartment where you don't know anybody and God knows what could happen to you."

"Don't be such a worrywart! It's time—past time. I'm twenty-eight years old. That's what people do. They find their own place."

"The restaurant was always good enough for us."

Guilt twisted in Poppy. "And I'm happy for you. But think about what you just said. The café was always your dream. Not mine."

"You have everything you need."

"Everything I have was given to me! Maybe I want to see if I can get something for myself."

"But why? That's all I'm asking."

Poppy whipped her head around to her mother.

"Because all my life, I've felt dumb. I failed kindergarten! Who does that? *Who fails kindergarten?*"

To her horror, Poppy realized her mistake the second it was out of her mouth. Mom had failed eleventh grade—and dropped out of high school.

In her haste to apologize, Poppy hopped up, forgetting about her heel.

"Ow!"

Her mom caught Poppy's flailing arm. "Now, see what I mean? Lucky I was here to catch you. But you know dyslexia does not mean you're dumb."

Poppy hugged her. "I know. I'm sorry."

Mom pulled out of her embrace while still holding on to her to keep her steady. "Your teacher told us that at that meeting, remember? The only reason they held you back was because you were a little behind on your reading."

A faraway look came into Mom's eyes. "It's too bad they didn't know more about learning disabilities back when I was in school. Sometimes I think your problem is all because of—what's the word?"

"Mom. No."

"Genes. That's it. And I gave it to you."

"It's not your fault."

"Being a waitress was all I ever did. But I was good at it. Your Pop and I worked hard to get the café up and running. Then when we saw the same problems cropping up in you that I had—trouble with reading, holding your pencil real awkward, like I do—we worked even harder. We always had it in the back of our minds that one day you could take over. Kind of like an insurance policy that you'd always have a job."

Poppy tried not to cry. Nothing her mom said was a surprise. But they didn't dwell on her disability. It had taken something like this to bring it out in the open again.

Mom broke the tension with a sniff and helped Poppy back to the couch.

"So. What are you going to do now?"

"Heath thinks I ought to ask Keval to shoot another practice session showing me doing something right, to vindicate myself."

"But, honey, won't you just be putting yourself out there all over again? Didn't you say it was live video?"

"I can rehearse without Keval, then invite him in when I'm comfortable."

Her mom clenched her hands until her knuckles were white. "I just hate to see you get hurt again, that's all."

"I can do this, Mom."

She brushed away a loose strand of hair from Poppy's face. "Sure you can, honey."

Poppy wished she sounded more convinced.

Chapter Seven

Heath walked into the low-slung rancher and set the little bag Scarlett Springer had given him on the kitchen table. An unyielding melancholy hung in the stale air.

"I'm home."

He stood still, waiting for a reply, but there was silence except for the ticking of the clock. If not for Heath changing the battery at the same time he changed the batteries in the smoke alarms, it would be long dead by now.

He deposited a sticky bun on each of two plates.

Dad wasn't in his workshop. That only left his recliner, in the den.

"Dad?"

Dad grunted without turning away from the Seahawks and 49ers. An afghan at least as old as Heath covered his legs.

"Sticky bun from Poppy's. Scarlett sent them over."

"Hntp."

Heath set the saucer on the arm of his dad's recliner and sat down on the couch next to him.

Dad kept the room so dim you could barely see the old family photos on the mantel, the wall hanging his mother had macraméed in better times.

"How come you got the curtains closed? It's nice out today."

Other than football, one of the few topics that interested Dad was the weather. It had to. His nursery stock depended on it.

"How long you been sitting there?"

His dad blinked and turned to him, as if just noticing his presence.

"Huh? I don't know. Hour or two."

"What's the score?"

"It was seven, thirteen a while ago."

"Did you eat anything today?"

"Some of that lunch meat that you bought."

The bomb thrown by the Seahawks quarterback was snatched one-handed from a near-interception by their receiver, who ran it in for a touchdown.

"Yes!" Heath jumped up from the couch. "You see that? Now for the extra point . . ."

As if he were in a trance, Dad chewed his sticky bun without replying.

Heath watched the kicked ball soar through the goalposts, polishing off his own bun. "These are good," he mumbled, licking his fingers. "I'm going to get a glass of milk. Want some?"

"Don't bother."

"No bother."

Dad's listlessness was nothing new. He'd been withdrawing deeper and deeper into himself for the past twenty years. Hard as Heath tried to interest him in the outside world, he could only do so much.

On his way to the kitchen he avoided looking down the hallway at two doors standing ajar. One of them led to Dad's room, once shared with Mom. And though it'd been years since Heath had set foot in there, he knew from passing by it on his way to the bathroom that the sagging mattress had the same blue printed bedspread on it that had been there when his mother left.

The opposite door led to the room that belonged to Heath and, back when they'd been a real family, his twin.

There was a time when Heath and Hayden had shared the same crib. They grew into toddlers and then rambunctious boys.

They ate, bathed, slept, and played together. They even wore matching clothes Mom bought them.

Heath still didn't know when he realized that he was the stronger of the two. For one thing, Hayden got tired before he did. If not that, it was the little bit of extra attention Mom gave Hayden.

But at least there was always someone to play with, talk to, and even huddle up with during thunderstorms in the blanket forts they made between the couches.

Heath grew stronger, but inexplicably, Hayden didn't. He used to be able to at least hold his own when they wrestled, even if nine times out of ten, Heath pinned him. But at some point he began getting breathless as soon as they got started.

By the time Hayden was diagnosed with leukemia, he had become too tired to wrestle at all. Heath would try to goad him into playing video games on the couch, but after a while even that became too much, and Mom shooed Heath away.

Before long their lives started to revolve around Hayden's doctor appointments, hospitalizations, special food, and worrisome phone calls overheard when Heath's parents thought he was out of earshot.

From the sidelines where he was shunted more and more, Heath sensed his parents' mounting fear and desperation as they became completely engrossed with his brother, to the exclusion of him.

One day, Hayden was hospitalized yet again. The next thing Heath knew, his grief-stricken parents were getting dressed up for something called a funeral. But Heath wasn't included. They said he was too young. Instead, they gave him a book. Something about angels and heaven. But when he asked Mom to read to him, she started crying again and left the room.

He was seven years old and full of questions. He missed his brother. He missed his parents.

His mom had stopped making meals for anyone but Hayden months ago. Dad went to work before Heath got up and came home after he had tucked himself into bed, only to stare at the empty one next to his in the gloom and wonder what had happened to the person once closest to him. Were they called still twin beds, if only one was occupied? Where was Hayden? Did he have a new bed, in that place called heaven?

Then, one morning, Heath was gently shaken awake to find Mom sitting on the edge of his bed, looking down at him. She brushed his hair out of his eyes and told him to get up and get dressed.

"What do you want for breakfast? I'll make you anything you want."

"Anything?"

With high hopes, he leapt out of bed, pulled on some shorts, and sat down to frozen waffles with chocolate syrup.

Mom hadn't been so attentive in weeks. Maybe the worst was over. Maybe things were going to get better now.

"Are we going to do something together?" There was a playground with a curving tunnel slide he really liked, a few minutes' drive away. He hadn't been there in a long time.

"We'll see."

The day was hot. Maybe they were going to the pool, Heath thought as he dutifully did as he was told and got into the car. But no, they didn't have their swimsuits or the beach bag.

Mom drove silently with Heath looking out the back window, searching for some clue as to their destination, until they pulled in along the curb on Main Street.

Then they went into Poppy's Café and Mom told Mrs. Springer she'd be back in a while.

He couldn't have known then that those were the last words he would ever hear his mother say.

Mrs. Springer's friendly smile and warm stickies smoothed over Heath's disheartened feelings. Mr. Springer let him hold the leaf blower when he swept the sidewalk in front of the café.

And then there was Poppy. She fascinated him, even if she *was* a girl. She was always babbling to her dolls or her parents or the customers or nobody at all. In fact, Poppy said more in five minutes than everyone in his house said in a whole day.

Midday, Mrs. Springer took Poppy and Heath back to their house so they could play outside for a while. Poppy collected an armful of dolls and accessories and he followed her out back where they sat down under the shade of a big tree. Poppy handed Heath a boy doll, then concocted an elaborate story about their dolls working at their own pretend café. It was kind of lame, but he went along with it. Nobody could see them anyway except Mrs. Springer, from her kitchen window where she washed the lunch dishes. Besides, playing dolls with Poppy distracted him from wondering where his own mom was and when she was coming back for him.

At suppertime, Mrs. Springer drove Heath and Poppy back to the café where she made them sandwiches and ice cream floats.

When the sun started setting outside the café windows and Mr. Springer said they were all going back to Poppy's house, Heath knew that something was terribly wrong.

That evening, Mr. Springer disappeared and came back with Heath's backpack filled with his pajamas and a fresh set of clothes.

Heath slept in the Springers' guest room for the rest of that week.

Finally, one day Dad's car pulled up outside Poppy's house.

Heath ran outside to meet him.

"Where's Mom?" he asked, dreading the answer, but frantic to know.

"We'll talk about it on the way home. Let's go in and get your stuff."

On their way back to their house, Heath asked him again.

"She was sad. She went away."

Heath choked back panic. "You mean like to heaven, to be with Hayden?"

"No. Just away, to be by herself for a while."

"But what about us? Doesn't she want to be with us?"

A tear slid down Dad's cheek. Dad never cried, not even when Hayden died. But now, the tears wouldn't stop.

"I don't understand," said Heath, alarmed. "When's she coming back?"

Dad pulled the car into the driveway and turned off the ignition.

"I don't know," he sobbed into his hands. "She left us. She's gone!"

He cried openly, in great, terrifying wails.

That's when Heath knew that someone would have to take control. And that that someone would have to be him.

He unclicked his seat belt, climbed out of the backseat and walked to the driver's door, opening it.

"It's okay," he said, his voice sounding small and inadequate for the monumental task he sensed loomed before him.

Now, a crowd cheer erupted from the TV in the den, bringing Heath back to the present.

He opened the fridge and got out the milk.

He had always been the strongest one. Stronger than Hayden, Mom, even his dad.

Heath went back to the den and handed his dad his glass.

"Hey, Dad. Our class reunion's coming up in December, at the Radish Rose. They want to borrow some saplings to dress it up. That okay? I'll help you with setup and takedown."

"Fine."

He planted his feet between the recliner and the TV. "Something else I wanted to mention. I know a guy who can get me fifty yard line seats for the Rams game, the week of Christmas. What do you think?"

Frowning, Dad craned his neck around Heath. "Get out of the way, would you? I don't know."

"We always talked about going up to Seattle to see a game. Let's do it."

"And get soaked? That's the height of the rainy season."

"I'll get us club seats, if you'd rather. They're all under cover."

"I'll let you know." He made a sweeping motion with his arm. "Now, get out of the way."

"Want me to throw together some supper in a while? A grilled cheese, some soup?"

He'd already eaten at the consortium, but he'd eat again if it meant some healthy interaction for Dad.

"No need." He finished the bun, brushed the crumbs away, and returned his blank stare to the TV.

Chapter Eight

On Thursdays after work, Heath went over to the consortium to compare industry notes with Sam. Their get-togethers had started organically, neither of them planning them. Now it was a weekly ritual both men looked forward to.

But for some reason, Sam had sent Heath a text asking him to stop by tonight, a Monday.

When Heath arrived, Sam wrapped his outstretched hand in both of his, creating a cocoon of trust. "Thanks for coming over, man." He poured Heath one of the special blends he kept under the counter for industry friends. "What've you got going this week?"

Heath held his wine up to the light, admiring its transparency. "The brew team's working on some R-and-D test batches for new production beers. You?"

"Couple of winemakers from over on Ribbon Ridge were in here blending this morning. A pianist from some big New York orchestra came in with her mother for a tasting. Said she was a guest performer at the symphony in Portland last weekend, and now they're spending the week doing the tourist thing."

"Guess you meet all kinds here."

"Wine lovers come from every walk of life. Those ladies really got a kick out of watching real winemakers sitting right over there, blending wines while they looked over their shoulders. But then, I hear hopheads are the same breed."

Heath tensed at what was coming.

"Craft beer has its own culture, too," said Sam. "But then, you know that. They're not the perma-drunks pounding growlers at some dive bar. They love to get together and talk about their new discoveries, compare old favorites, different processes."

"You and John. He doesn't miss a chance to tell me how I should be opening up a tasting room."

"I know you don't get off on schmoozing with strangers. But people are into the real deal. They love getting a tour from someone who just finished eight hours with their hands in the actual process, instead of some tour guide."

Heath tapped his fingers on the bar to the tune of the soft background music. Sooner or later Sam would open up about the real reason why he'd texted him to stop by.

"How's Poppy's foot? Sorry about that whole thing. I feel bad that it happened at my place."

"Got a few stitches to remember it by, but she'll be all right."

"Keval's video was a big hit while it lasted."

Heath looked up. "It's gone?"

"He set it up to disappear after a certain length of time, but get ready. He wants more. Says fresh content keeps people coming back for updates."

"Poppy said you'll let her do a blind tasting here. Any way we could come in and practice—without prying eyes?"

"I owe her, after what happened yesterday. How about Friday night, after closing? You can have the whole place to yourself. I'll show you how to lock up when you're done."

"You'll keep it on the down low? We'll let Keval in another time, after Poppy feels more confident."

"Keep what?" Sam grinned conspiratorially.

Heath nodded his thanks. "Nowadays there are cameras everywhere."

"Smart move. It wouldn't be good to have a repeat of that last performance."

Heath thought about Poppy's progress—and the lack of it—while he finished his wine.

Sam grabbed a different bottle and yanked out the cork. "See what you think of this one." He poured an ounce into a fresh glass and slid it in front of Heath.

It would be rude to turn down Sam's hospitality, but from here on out Heath was going to make use of the spit bucket. He wanted to have his wits about him when Sam finally got around to telling him what was on his mind.

He tasted the deep ruby liquid while Sam watched and waited for his verdict.

"Bright fruit nose. Chewy finish."

Sam nodded. "Not bad, eh? So, back to Poppy." He hesitated, choosing his words carefully. "You two ever . . . ?" He half grinned and shrugged.

A savage possessiveness seized Heath. Sam was interested in Poppy! That's what he wanted to talk about. He wanted to feel Heath out.

Fighting a wave of panic, Heath threw back his glass, gulped its contents, and wiped his mouth on the back of his hand.

Sam laughed. "I'll take that as a no."

This is Poppy we're talking about! How could Sam be so blasé?

But then, what right did Heath have to be mad?

"Poppy and I are friends. Nothing but friends."

Heath's heart pounded in his ears. Sam had always had a knack for reading people. He was even sharper after he came back from the service, a fact that only gave credence to the spy rumors floating around.

He took a steadying breath and looked down at where his fingers played with the base of his glass. "Why? What's it to you?"

"It's not such an off-the-wall question," said Sam mildly. "I don't know any red-blooded male who'd kick Poppy Springer out of bed. I mean, just picture the woman."

But Heath didn't think in pictures. His inner world was made up of smells and flavors, sounds and tactile sensations.

He flashed back to Poppy's hot little hand tugging his toward a squawking crowd of party guests . . . the salty-sweet tang of French fries dipped in catsup on his tongue, her nonstop chatter coming from across a cool Formica table in his ears. Then there was the heady perfume of lilacs by the creek that ninth-grade spring when he had drawn her initials in the dirt with the toe of his sneaker.

"Relax. Poppy Springer might be hotter than a stolen Ferrari, but she's not what I wanted to talk to you about tonight."

He looked up. "Then what?"

"I'm always looking for new ways to promote the consortium."

Heath was almost overcome with relief. *That's what this is about? Advertising?*

"We're doing well, but we're still new, and there're a lot of wineries where people can go to taste wine besides here. Ever hear of an outfit called Brides for a Cause? It's a charity that resells donated gowns at a huge discount. They donate the proceeds to engaged couples facing a serious illness or other tough circumstances.

"Holly and Keval cooked up the idea to host a fashion show. Could bring in customers that might not find us any other way, plus help a few needy folks. Keval thinks it'd be a slam dunk."

Heath was still recovering from shock, but it wouldn't do to let Sam see. "Poppy said something about a fashion show. You want me to contribute the beer."

It was no secret that Heath donated a good chunk of his profits to several local charities in memory of his twin.

"Or you could model a penguin suit. Your choice."

"Parade down a catwalk in a tux?" He sniffed. "Put me down for the beer."

Sam thrust out his hand. "Thanks, man. Knew I could count on you. I know you're not a limelight kind of guy, but you can still come watch if you want."

"When is it?" Heath asked, with no intention whatsoever of going to a fashion show, charity or not.

"Third Saturday in October."

"I think I have something that day," he lied as he slid his empty toward Sam.

"How do you know, if I'm not even sure of the date? Tell you what. Next time you see Dr. Red, ask her to confirm. She's volunteered to run it."

"You and Red seem to be in the same place at the same time quite a bit lately."

Sam averted his eyes and shook his head. "Doc just happened to be available. Think about it. Who's got more empathy for people in crisis than a therapist?"

"I guess." Heath slid off his stool and headed for the exit. "Thanks for the wine."

"Any time. Oh—by the way, did I mention? Poppy's going to be playing the role of the bride."

Heath fought to keep his voice casual. "Oh yeah? Who's the groom?"

"Not that it matters, because you and Poppy are just friends, right?"

"Who is it?" Heath wouldn't be able to rest until he knew.

"Daryl Decaprio."

Heath felt the corner of his mouth twitch.

"That's right." Sam chuckled. "Clarkston's answer to Brad Pitt— or so say the ladies. Hell—don't listen to them. You were at the last Splash party. Dude is shredded, man. Gotta give him props. There's one high school quarterback that never went soft."

The thought of Daryl's brawny build at last summer's pool party made Heath's own average biceps flex involuntarily.

"Yeah, Poppy and Decaprio will be declaring their vows right . . . over . . . *there*." He squinted and pointed to the far end of the consortium's main public room as if aiming a gun. "Even renting a portable stage." He picked up a rag and wiped a spot on the bar. "Didn't have to ask him twice. Then again, Decaprio is known for having the biggest"—Sam rinsed out his rag, pausing over the sound of running water—"*ego* west of the Mississippi. Should be quite a show. 'Course, like I said, it's all for a good cause."

Chapter Nine

I don't know any red-blooded male who'd kick Poppy Springer out of bed. All you have to do is picture the woman.

For the rest of that week, Sam's words dogged Heath. Hell, wasn't his blood as red as the next guy's? Yet he had never thought of Poppy as merely a face . . . a collection of body parts, let alone someone he wanted to sleep with. To him, she was just . . . Poppy.

Tuesday, while he tasted batches of research and development ales, he ran through the mental list of women he'd been with over the last couple of years.

Okay, so maybe he wouldn't win any skirt-chasing contests. If he were honest, every woman he'd been with had come on to *him*, not the other way around. And none of those women had managed to rope him into more than a few dates, though a couple had been pretty persistent. But he had a good excuse. He'd been a tad busy managing the mushrooming growth of his company.

Wednesday, he sat down with his brew team. While he half listened to their debate grow heated over when to clear out tank space for the next beer coming down the line, a haphazard progression of Poppy impressions swam in his head. Her gap-toothed grin in fourth grade, a lopsided headband she'd made from a fistful of wilted flowers he'd thrust at her. Years later, downcast gray eyes whenever Ms. Baker called on her to parse sentences at the whiteboard. Even now, his heart still clutched at the injustice of her being forced to stand up there long after she was humiliated and the other kids were squirming in embarrassment for her.

When it came right down to it, the place where Poppy had always looked most at home was the café. Her smile lit up the room and her cheerful service kept patrons coming back.

Thursday, as he skimmed over marketing's short list of names for next year's winter seasonal beer, he tried to reconcile the current Poppy with his original perception of her. At what age had he first realized their differences? It was around the time when his voice started cracking and hair started sprouting in embarrassing places on his body. Around the same time she'd sat cross-legged across from him on a beach towel at the Clarkston Pool, all jutting knees and pointy elbows and a purple swimsuit, soundly beating him at a game of Set. Fast forward to last weekend, up in his tree house. The soft, warm sensation of two small mounds pressing against his chest when she'd thrown herself at him had his body reacting all over again.

"Boss?"

"Huh?" At the head of the conference table, Heath shifted his weight in his chair.

"The new winter beer. Chillsner or Christmas Bonus?"

"Sorry. How 'bout you guys take a vote. We'll go with whatever name wins."

Finally it was Friday, the day he'd been looking forward to all week. Tonight, he was determined to look at Poppy through new eyes—red-blooded, male eyes. He had all evening to conduct a thorough, scientific examination of her. Methodically, starting at the top and working his way down.

It was dusk when he picked Poppy up at her parents' house.

She launched into a monologue about her week the moment he let her in his car, only pausing while he walked around and got into the driver's seat. Once Poppy got rolling, there was no need to be an active participant. A nod here, a "really?" there was all she required.

While she bantered, he tried to pinpoint exactly what it was about her unique aroma that impacted him so powerfully.

He'd actually taken time from some pressing brewery issues to research the subject of scent. Starting with orange blossom, technically neroli. Sweet, floral, and slightly haunting. Papers had been written about its antimicrobial and antibacterial properties, and there were fascinating hypotheses hinting that more beneficial substances may yet be found in it.

". . . Sandy and Kyle let it be known that they're planning to name their baby boy Hawthorne?" Poppy's voice rose in a question. "What do you think of that? Not that there's anything wrong with it. Hawthorne is a perfectly good name. I'm just not sure how well it goes with Houser. Hawthorne Houser..."

Jasmine. Mostly benzyl and acetate. Exotic and rich. Deeply relaxing, some claimed it was an aphrodisiac.

The words "Poppy" and "aphrodisiac" in the same sentence sent his thoughts careening down unfamiliar roads with dangerous curves and sharp drop-offs.

When he read that sandalwood also was associated with the awakening of sexual energies, he had gotten off the web and back onto his spreadsheet of shipping dates and tank space. All that aphrodisiac talk was purely speculative. There was no hard scientific evidence that aphrodisiacs were even a real thing.

"...the new dress Junie had on the other day. You know Junie hardly ever wears dresses."

"Really?"

"In fact, now that I think about it, the only dress I can remember seeing Junie in is that yellow sundress she wore to the Clarkston Splash last year. Remember that one? It went straight across at the bust and then flared out to a modified A-line..."

They pulled into the consortium to see Sam standing in the doorway, saying good-bye to his last customers of the day.

Inside, Sam cheerfully told Poppy to get lost until he'd shown Heath what he had prepared for the blind tasting.

"C'mon back," he said, motioning for Heath to follow him behind the bar. "I'll show you what we've got."

Poppy meandered around the room, studying the black-and-white photos of local landscapes on the walls while Sam showed Heath the row of brown paper bags sitting upright on the counter, the numbers one through six written on them with a Sharpie.

"Three reds, three whites," said Sam. "Poppy and I settled up earlier." He reached into his pocket and flipped him a key to the building. "Here you go. Have fun. Lock her up when you're done."

"Thanks for letting us use the room," Poppy called as Sam headed toward the door and she drifted over to the bar.

"You kids be good." Sam winked and was gone.

Poppy's scent swirled around Heath. "Is it warm in here?" he asked, looking around for the thermostat.

"It feels almost chilly to me," Poppy replied, rubbing her arms.

No wonder the woman was cold. She had on a sleeveless cropped top that showed a horizontal slice of her lumbar region above her jeans when she sat down.

Heath took off his leather jacket and slung it across the bar. "Here. You need this more than I do."

She shivered as she slipped her arms into the sleeves. "It's different here with no one else around," she said, her eyes flitting from the bar to the seating alcoves furnished with inviting couches and chairs. "Quiet."

"We have the whole building to ourselves—for the rest of the night, if we want. Not that we would *want* to—" he hastened to add.

Poppy propped her chin on her hand and looked at him mischievously. "Want to what?"

Feeling his cheeks redden, he turned his attention to the task at hand. He numbered square white bar napkins to match the wine sacks with the Sharpie he found next to the cash register and found six glasses.

"Are you going to have some?" asked Poppy, watching him pour.

"I'll try a little."

He had to keep a clear head. Not because he was proctoring her. He wouldn't have any trouble with that. He wanted to stay sober so he could study her objectively while she was preoccupied with analyzing the wines.

He sat the samples on the correspondingly numbered napkins.

Poppy gave him a stack of worksheets. "As soon as I touch the first glass, start the timer. For each wine, I'll say something about the appearance, nose, palate, and so on. Check the box next to each characteristic I mention. In twenty-five minutes, stop me."

Heath pulled up the timer on his cell phone and poised his thumb above it. "Whenever you're ready."

She settled into her seat and said, "Go."

Heath hit the timer in the same second Poppy picked up the first glass, inserted her nose into the bowl, and sniffed.

"Wine number one is a straw-color wine of low intensity, low nose."

She raised the glass to her lips and drank.

And then she started rattling off adjectives at warp speed.

"Fruits are green apple, yellow pear, honeydew melon rind. Non-fruit characteristics include vegetal and herbal. Structure is moderately acidic. This wine is from a moderately cool climate. The primary grape is Pinot Grigio, Old World style. Country of origin is Italy. Age is one to three years. Final conclusion, this is a two thousand thirteen pinot grigio from Alto Adige in Italy."

"Hold on—" he said, his eyes zigzagging frantically across the page, still looking for the word "structure."

"Wine number two is an opaque purple color. Intense aromas of smoke, black raspberries, and spice. Tannins soft and integrated, low acidity—"

"Slow down."

"—full-bodied with an unctuous texture and an expansive mid-palate. Alcohol is high. Final conclusion, this is a red blend from the Southern Rhone of France. Nineteen ninety-five Châteauneuf-du-Pape."

Poppy continued at a breakneck pace until she'd whizzed through all the entries, only hesitating once to go back and change an original conclusion.

It seemed like no time at all until she sat down the sixth glass and sat back. "Stop!"

Heath glanced at his phone, stunned. "You still have four minutes to go."

"I'm through. How many did I get right?" Impatiently, she reached for the first bag and pulled the bottle out. "Pinot grigio! Yay!"

"I didn't catch half your descriptors. You were flying."

"The descriptors are just a means to an end. I'm mainly concerned with my conclusions." She stooped over the bar, trying to read upside down the grids he'd marked.

"I'll come over there," said Heath.

When he got around the bar he noticed that his jacket didn't quite cover up that slice of skin on her lower back. He stepped into the space between her stool and the one next to it and bowed his head next to hers, skimming over her results with her.

"I got five right out of six!"

Heath was more surprised that she was. "That's really—"

But Poppy cut him off mid-sentence, throwing herself into his arms for the second time in a week.

Any red-blooded man would squeeze her back.

And that's what Heath did.

But a mere second later she extricated herself and started bouncing on the bar stool, chanting, "Oh yeah! Oh yeah!" Her eyes flew open wide. "That's what we need—music!"

She dove for her bag, whipped out her phone, and hopped off the bar stool. "Come on!" she called with a toss of her head. "Let's dance!"

He caught a glimpse of skin, a flash of navel inside his jacket.

And that's when his earlier objective to methodically analyze her flew out the window. This wasn't the little girl he once knew. *This* Poppy was every inch a woman. When had that happened? How had he been so blind, and for how long?

And then her weight landed on her heel and her knee buckled. In the blink of an eye her jubilant expression turned tortured, and she inhaled sharply.

Before he knew what he was doing he was there, his arm snaking around her waist, propping her up. "Over here." He guided her toward the nearest couch, letting her use his body as a crutch.

"If I hadn't second-guessed myself, I would have gotten all six of those wines right!" said Poppy. Not even her pain could erase her elation for long. For Poppy, every victory, even a small one, was cause for celebration.

But for Heath, that test was rapidly becoming a memory.

The main thing is her foot and easing her discomfort, insisted his ever-practical nature.

He tried to maintain decorum as he deposited her rump onto a couch covered in a crimson plush and, mission accomplished, began to straighten his spine.

But Poppy apparently had a different idea. Still caught up in her enthusiasm, she seemed to be in no hurry to unclamp her grip from around his neck.

With a growing uncertainty, Heath searched her face and saw that now her expression had softened. Her eyes sparkled with a new ardor that both disturbed and exhilarated him. A waterfall of gold cascaded behind her as her head fell back, exposing her vulnerable neck, her eyes narrowed, and her lips parted in invitation.

He was helpless to resist her. One of his hands reached around to support her nape while the other cupped her cheek. His pulse raced, his breath came in a rush from his nostrils, as inch by inch, the space between their lips closed.

And then he was lost in the scent of orange blossoms, the hot, slippery warmth of her mouth, the curve of her waist. His heart pounded, creating a warm flush starting in the center of his chest, spreading outward.

Poppy arched her body up toward his in a wantonness that both shocked and thrilled him. His scalp tingled where her fingers raked through his hair, which he was always forgetting to get cut.

The kiss deepened, changed angles as chins and tongues jockeyed to get closer . . . ever closer. And then she was reclining back along the length of the couch, taking him with her.

Pulled off balance, one of his knees landed between hers. A hand landed next to her ear and the fingers of the other slid into the crack between the cushions as he braced his weight above her.

But far from being daunted at the prospect of being crushed, she seemed to beg for it. She tugged on his torso and squirmed until she was directly under him, as if desperate to feel his length along hers.

In a voice thick with emotion, he choked out a hoarse warning. "Poppy . . ."

"Huhhhh?" she breathed. In her eyes was a message even a boy could recognize.

Step aside—I'll take it from here, said the red-blooded male to the scientist in Heath.

He was the victim of her whim, led by swelling desire until he was fully submerged in a blur of hands and tastes and the sound of skin brushing against skin.

As the breaking point threatened with the impact of a runaway train, Heath caught a glimpse of the brown bags containing the wine bottles sitting on the bar, and in a flash of sanity, he remembered why they were there.

Bracing himself on one hand, he frowned down at her, panting.

"What?" she asked, frustrated.

When he couldn't immediately verbalize an answer, she lost patience and cupped the back of his head, greedily pulling him down for more.

But again he cut the kiss short.

"We can't."

Carefully, he disengaged from where they lay entangled and stood up, tucking his shirt into his pants. Before he'd even had time to catch his breath he walked away with lead in his shoes, scrubbing a hand through his hair, not trusting himself to turn around again until he had put the bar between them.

Poppy had propped herself up on one elbow, frowning. "What's the matter?"

Heath looked longingly at the rapid rise and fall of her chest... her breasts cradled in her snowy-white bra, the gentle swell of her belly where it disappeared into unzipped jeans, and every hormone and muscle in his body screamed to go back over there and finish what they had started.

"I'm supposed to be helping you move away from Clarkston."

And you're making me want you to stay, he thought.

Mechanically, his hands found wineglasses and the faucet handle and dish soap. They itched for action, and he had to occupy them *some* way.

After a minute or so, from the vicinity of the couch came the swish of fabric and the rasp of a zipper closing.

He looked up from throwing away the numbered bags to see Poppy once again across the bar from where he stood, looking sheepish.

She ran her fingers through her long hair and looked down at the sparkling bar surface that Heath continued to wipe. "I don't know what to say."

Well, if Poppy Springer was at a loss for words, *he* was too.

Poppy's head spun. She was as surprised as Heath when she'd thrown herself at him. What had come over her? Getting physical would set them up for complications neither one needed. It was a bad move.

Dumb.

If her pride had been hurt when he pushed her away, she had only herself to blame.

She went over to the bar where Heath was. "I wasn't thinking. I was just...*feeling*...celebrating the test results. That's all."

Heath finally stopped cleaning and sucked in an audible breath.

"Why are you really doing this? What's the big deal about becoming a sommelier? Why isn't Clarkston good enough for you?"

"You too?" she snapped, thinking of her mom's lack of faith in her, despite her declaration of support. "You've got some nerve! No one has ever questioned *your* goals. No one asked *you* why you wanted to become a brewer." Her palm came down on the bar and she leaned toward him accusingly. "Why is everyone questioning mine? Aren't I allowed to reach for my potential, just like everyone else?"

She knew she wasn't being fair, taking out her fear of failure on him, but she couldn't stop herself. He was a safe target. She trusted him not to hold it against her.

"I didn't say that."

"That's what it sounded like."

She slouched again and frowned, anxiously fingering a lock of hair, the sound of her breath rushing through her nostrils filling her head.

And then Heath was coming around the bar with long strides.

Instantly he was next to her, his thigh touching her knee.

"You're good at the café," he pleaded. "It works. People like you here. They . . ." He pressed his lips together. "Love you."

She scowled defiantly. "Who loves me?"

He shifted uncomfortably, unable—or unwilling—to elaborate. "You know."

"No. I don't," she said, egging him on insolently.

What is wrong with me? She knew he wasn't good with explanations.

"Tell me who loves me."

What do I want from him?

"Well," he fumbled, "all your customers at the café."

"The customers. Well, *that's* enough to build a life on," she spat acerbically.

"Yeah. They're always talking about how good you are at, you know, things."

"What things?"

"You know. Pouring coffee." He brightened. "Remembering their orders without writing them down."

"Remembering orders. You think there's a category for that in *The Guinness Book of World Records*? I'll have to check and see."

"How about your parents, then? They love you."

She tsked and rolled her eyes in derision. "Of *course* my parents love me. Don't everyone's?"

A second too late, she remembered. She might not be the most successful person in Clarkston, but at least she had grown up with the knowledge that she was wanted. That was more than Heath had.

Heath looked away, and Poppy knew that last comment was beyond the pale. Filled with regret, she laid her hand on his arm. "I'm sorry."

Shrugging her off, he turned and paced a few steps, hands on his hips, distancing himself from her insensitivity. "Forget it."

She hopped off her stool, winced, and kept going despite the pain. "Heath. I didn't mean to hurt your feelings. I would never do that."

He turned back around, his face a careful blank. "I said, don't worry about it."

He was so good and kind and generous to her, and she was such a jerk. Somehow, she had to make him understand what she was going through, but how could she when she didn't understand it herself?

She pleaded with her eyes. "Every one of our friends will have some accomplishment to talk about at the ten-year reunion except me—which is exactly what Demi predicted. Do you know what that means? How that makes me feel about myself?" No sooner had she reached for the tips of her hair than she started chastising herself for her old, childish habit, one she was ready to lose. She tossed her mane back over her shoulder where she wouldn't be tempted.

And then she realized she was crying.

Heath rushed to snatch a tissue from a nearby cocktail table and pressed it into her hand.

She honked into it a few times while he wore a worried expression.

"Look," he said. "Let's pretend this never happened."

"How am I supposed to do that?" she asked, wiping her nose.

"We'll just keep working on your exam, like before."

"You're going to keep helping me, even though you don't want me to do it." She huffed a sad laugh at the irony. "*That's* not hypocritical or anything."

"Go ahead, call me a hypocrite. All I know is, I can't stand it if we're not okay."

She blew her nose once more and handed him back the soggy tissue, which he took without flinching.

She sniffed, mulling it over.

"Okay," she said, calmer now. "I couldn't stand that, either."

Chapter Ten

Armed with her knowledge of the doctor's orders—*thanks, Heath*—there was no way Mom was going to let Poppy go in to work for the next week. And after Mom told Big Pop, it was two against one.

Her father patted Poppy on the back on his way to work each morning, while Mom brought her tea and fluffed up the pillow under her foot and watched Poppy struggle with her mysterious exam notes, the faithful Jackson curled up on the carpet by her side.

By day six, Poppy was bored and lonely. When Red texted to ask if she'd be in to work, she told her yes and then used that as an excuse to get Mom to cave.

Poppy was relieved to see Red breeze in to the warm café, rosy from her short walk from her office in the brisk autumn air.

"You're back! I've been wanting to catch you up on the fashion show."

Poppy showed Red to a booth and slid in across from her.

"What have I missed while I've been in prison?" asked Poppy.

Red unwound her wool scarf and set it on the seat beside her. "First things first. Do I still have my bride?"

"Of course. Ready to roll." Poppy stuck her foot out to the side of the booth so Red could see it.

"No more bandage?"

"Bandage gone, the stitches dissolved."

"Thank goodness. I figure two rehearsals will be enough, don't you? One without the dresses and one after they've been delivered?"

"You're the director. Just let me know when to be there. I would have been back to work even sooner if it weren't for the warden lady." She tossed her head toward her mom, who was chatting with a customer at the register.

Red chuckled. "Doing hard time in the big house, huh?"

"You have no idea. Thank goodness for your text. I got paroled a day early."

"Poppy's isn't the same when you're not here. It's good to see you back."

"Not as good as it is for me to see you. I'm dying to talk to someone born after nineteen sixty. Plus, I just drank three cups of Stumptown's Costa Rican."

"I'd think it would be nice, having your mom pamper you when you're laid up."

Poppy sighed. "I don't mean to sound ungrateful. My parents are the best. I'm just tired of being treated like an eight-year-old."

"That why you're ready to move out?"

Poppy rested her head in her hands. "I can't believe I've never lived anywhere but with my parents."

"Everybody progresses as her own rate."

"I don't know what's taken me so long."

"You grew up in a safe, cozy nest. People need a deep inner motivation to justify moving out. Maybe you're just now finding that."

"That's exactly it. Before I was promoted to manager of the wine shop and passed my first sommelier test, I didn't think I had it in me to ever do anything but work here, at the café."

"It takes some people longer than others to tap into their passions, build up momentum and get enough confidence to strike out on their own."

"Excuse me," called Demi Barnes from the opposite side of the café. "Are you working? We could use a refill over here."

"Another reunion meeting," Poppy sighed. "Be right back."

When Poppy returned a minute later Red asked, "What are you hearing about the reunion?"

"Did you know the theme is Bacchanalia?"

"That's fitting, given the valley's the new home of pinot noir. Though those ancient Romans did tend to get a little off the chain when they partied."

"Off the chain?"

"Orgies, binges lasting for days. Nothing was sacred. Speaking of off the chain, what about you and Demi? Are things civil between you two?"

"You mean since I sprayed her with champagne?" She smirked self-effacingly. "Some sommelier I'm going to make."

Red giggled. "I shouldn't laugh. But Demi has such a superiority complex. It was kind of satisfying to see her brought down a peg."

"I thought she'd tear into me the next time she saw me, but she acted as though it never happened."

"She doesn't have to milk that," said Red. "Not when she's got these ongoing reunion meetings here, where you have no choice but to defer to her."

"What do you mean?"

"Why do you think she decided to switch meeting locations as soon as she found out you were back working here? So she could flaunt her power over you."

Poppy frowned. "But Demi has everything going for herself. A prestigious job, brains, great organizational skills . . . why's she have to be so mean?"

Calmly, Red sipped her coffee. "She's jealous of you."

"*Please.* Because Daryl used to play me songs on the phone when we were, what? Fourteen?" Poppy made a face. "I didn't even know Demi liked him, or I wouldn't have taken his calls. It didn't mean anything. It was just kid stuff. Mildly interesting, at the most."

"No. Because you were so effortlessly popular, all through school. Everybody liked you without you even trying. That gave you power, in her eyes. Power that she craved."

Poppy shrugged. "I like people. If they like me back, all the better."

"I know. You're self-referring."

"You're losing me with your therapist talk."

"If you're not happy about something in your life, you look to make a change in *yourself.* You don't crave control over others. You're so different from someone like Demi, you can't even fathom how she operates.

"What about the reunion? You think any more about going?"

Poppy sat back, putting distance between her and Red. She knew shouldn't let an old senior superlative get to her. But these days, she was touchy about the slightest suggestion of what she should and shouldn't do.

"I have other things on my plate. I'm trying to block it out of my head. I'm sure there's a fancy psychological term for that."

"Let's see. Maybe . . . avoidance behavior?"

Poppy pointed at Red. "Yeah. Sounds about right. Anyway, I'm going to concentrate on passing my test."

"When is it?"

"Two days before the reunion."

She chewed her lower lip.

"How's the studying going?"

"Heath's been coaching me."

Red eyed her sideways.

"Why are you looking at me like that?"

"Like what?"

"Like you're analyzing me."

Red smiled slyly. "I don't know what you're talking about. You're my friend, not my client."

"Okay, friend. How come you're acting like something's going on between me and Heath?"

"Is there?"

"No! Heath and I are just friends. That's all we've ever been." The memory of throwing herself at Heath, and him pushing her away, popped into her head, reviving that uneasy feeling.

"I can still remember you and Heath hanging out here at the café after school when we were little. Seemed like you two were always together."

"It worked for everyone concerned. Mom and Big Pop ran the café all by themselves back then. They couldn't afford a sitter. Heath tolerated my prattle—kept me occupied while my parents worked. And as much as he went through, he was never any trouble. But you know Heath."

"Hayden's death had to have been a seminal event in his life," said Red.

"And then losing his mom, on top of that . . . I never understood how she could do that. Just . . . leave, and never come back."

"The death of a child is one of the worst kinds of loss."

"I still don't understand. Why couldn't his parents comfort each other?"

"You would think that would come naturally, wouldn't you? Often it doesn't, though, even in a healthy marriage. It can be like leaning on someone who's already doubled over in pain."

"But how can a mother be so distraught she walks away from her remaining child?" Poppy shook her head. *Especially a precious little boy like Heath.* "That's what I don't get."

"Everyone grieves differently. I can only presume that she shut down in self-defense. There could be another factor in play, too. It's not often talked about, but multiple births can be exceptionally stressful. So stressful that parents of twins sometimes have more trouble bonding with them than parents of singles."

"I can't put myself in Heath's mom's shoes. All I know is, losing her right after losing his twin had to have been hurtful and confusing. I've always wondered if that's why he isn't real outgoing."

"He could be a bit of a natural introvert. But there's something else, something I think you should know."

Poppy found that she was holding her breath.

"Children who are abandoned, like Heath was, can grow up believing they're not lovable."

"Heath? Not lovable? That's crazy." *What's not to love?* He was perfect. Cute, genius smart, always put her needs before his.

"At the very least, they find it hard to trust. One thing I know for sure..."

"What's that?" Nervously, she fingered the tips of her hair, picturing Heath's dear face with the perpetual worry frown lines between his brows.

"Heath Sinclair trusts you."

"Well, of course he trusts me. I trust him, too."

Red spread her hands on the table and studied her crimson manicure. "What I'm trying to say is, it's going to be hard for him to see you go in December. You are—you always have been—one of the most consistent, reliable forces in his life."

Poppy squirmed. She was starting to wonder a wee, tiny bit how she would do without Heath, too.

Maybe that was why she'd thrown herself at him at the consortium. Maybe she had to see what it felt like to push the boundaries of their relationship, before it was too late.

"I'll only be an hour away, you know."

"But from what Keval said, it sounds as though you're going to have a packed schedule, what with the modeling, the traveling, and the wine steward job."

"I've been working in Portland for the past few years."

"But you still came home to Clarkston every night. You can see why, in Heath's perception, you never really left."

"There were *weeks* when Heath and I didn't run into each other. I might as well have been living in another town."

"But the fact is, you weren't. If Heath had needed you, *really* needed you any time in the past few years, he knew where to find you. This . . . this is the real deal. There will be times when you're unreachable. Stretches when you can't drop everything and run back to Clarkston. For all intents and purposes, you're going to be gone from Heath's life, for good."

Worry made her hackles rise again. "Why is everyone giving me a hard time about moving on with my life?"

Across the room, Demi looked up at Poppy's outburst.

Red laid her hand on Poppy's and lowered her voice a notch. "Who's giving you a hard time? You deserve this. I couldn't be happier for you. But you know as well as I do that you're going to get caught up in your new life. Your old life will gradually fall away. That's just the way things work."

Red's disturbing prediction was tempered by her calm delivery, helping Poppy to keep her head.

"Heath's not the only one I'll be leaving behind. Everyone I care about is in Clarkston: Junie, Keval. You."

"Do you have a place to live lined up?"

Thank goodness Red was veering the conversation toward more practical matters. She dropped her split ends and sat on her hands to keep from picking them up again.

"I went apartment shopping online while I was laid up. I made a couple of appointments in the Arts District for next Sunday."

"Ooh! House hunting is my favorite hobby. And I've been wanting to stop by Brides for a Cause again before the fashion show. We have too many narrow skirts. I like the big, puffy numbers."

Poppy made a face. "Really? Those remind me of those over-the-top Gypsy weddings on that TV show. The straight ones are more elegant."

"You just haven't seen the right ones yet."

"Well, it's not like I'm in the market."

"I love looking at gowns almost as much as I like house hunting."

"Brides for a Cause is in the Arts District."

Red put a finger to her lips and thought. "That's right—it is!"

"Want to come with me?"

Chapter Eleven

On Sunday, Red called Poppy while she was getting ready to leave for Portland.

"I mentioned to Sam that I was making a trip to Brides for a Cause, and he asked if he could tag along. Maybe we should go separately? I don't want to hijack your whole day."

"Not a problem. Should I still pick you up at the café?"

"Sam said he would drive us in the van, in case I saw more dresses I want to bring back for the show. We can pick you up at your house."

"What about the apartments?"

"Sam's curious, too. He said he wouldn't mind ferrying you around."

"Even better. It won't hurt to have a few extra opinions before I sign a lease on something."

But no sooner had Poppy climbed in behind Sam and fastened her seat belt than she was startled to see they were pulling into Heath's driveway. She was even more surprised to see Heath standing outside, waiting.

"I didn't know Heath was coming." The last time they'd been together, she'd made a fool of herself by lunging at him, then picking a fight. The idea of spending the whole day with him stirred up her emotions all over again.

But the situation was out of her control. She wasn't driving, and there were other people to consider.

"I've been trying to lasso him to get him up to the city for a while," said Sam. "Couple of brewpubs I want to take him to, and I thought, the more the merrier. After your appointments, that is."

After a pit stop for coffees, Poppy did her best not to look at

Heath, catty-corner from her in the front seat, close enough to touch. But hard as she tried to focus on Red's chatter about the upcoming fashion show, billowy skirts, and the ideal wine to serve at a wedding, she couldn't stop stealing glances at the curve of his shoulder, the way his soft brown hair waved over the top of his ear.

What was pegged as an hour's drive turned into ninety minutes, thanks to highway construction to widen the main road between the city and the wine country to accommodate the growing numbers of tourists and the resultant explosion in the size and number of suburbs. Finally, Sam slowed the van along a city street.

"We must be close," said Poppy. "There's the liquor store the Realtor said was on the same corner as the apartment."

Sam rolled around the block a couple of times before he found a place to park. Then the four of them followed the waiting real estate agent up a flight of stairs to the first apartment on Poppy's list. The price was right, and the wall color was a nice, neutral beige that would go with anything.

But as the Realtor was showing Poppy how to operate the window blinds, they heard shouts coming from outside.

"Stop! Police!"

Poppy peered out the window and saw a man clutching a bottle, tearing down the sidewalk from the direction of the liquor store with a cop in hot pursuit.

"Someone's thirsty," said Sam calmly, over her shoulder.

"Or he stole that bottle of tequila," said Poppy indignantly.

Sam gave her an amazed look. "Ya think?"

Poppy felt herself blush at her naiveté.

After that, she didn't hear another word the Realtor said. Between Red giving her the hairy eyeball, Heath suddenly glued to her side, and Sam prowling around outside like he was her personal protection officer or something, she had all she could do just to let him finish his spiel.

The second stop was a new, gated community of cottage-style town houses. Poppy and Red oohed and aahed over the marble counters, spacious bath, and fenced-in, postage-stamp backyard.

Heath said nothing.

"You're quiet," said Poppy when Red and Sam had drifted off to look at the second bedroom. Even quieter than usual.

"How am I supposed to get in a word edgewise?"

She laughed. "I know. When Red and I get to talking, especially when you add caffeine to the mix . . ."

She spun around in the middle of the living room.

"Isn't this cute, though? Safe area, washer/dryer . . ."

"Hnmpt." The fine line between his brows deepened. "There's no creek to cool your toes in on a hot afternoon. No sound of the breeze blowing through the treetops."

She planted her hands on her hips. "You have to admit, it's better than the last one."

"Anything's better than the last one. But you're the one who's searching. It's whatever makes you happy."

How could I have thought this would work—both of us pretending nothing is amiss? Heath backing her self-improvement quest was already too much without rubbing his nose in the reality of her starting over, far away. His coming here today was bound to ratchet up the tension between them.

At Brides for a Cause, Red introduced Sam to one of the managers while Poppy skimmed through dress racks just for fun and Heath checked out a nearby garden shop.

Red picked out some fuller dresses for the fashion show, and Sam and Poppy helped her load them, bagged in plastic, into the van.

They were parched by the time Sam ushered them into a wood-heavy space with faux Tiffany lamps hanging overhead.

"Check out their formula, man," Sam told Heath. "They're keeping it simple. Five homebrews, five sandwiches. And when the Blazers are playing, they pack 'em in with ten-dollar pitchers."

"Let's give their sampler plate a try," said Heath. "I'm buying."

"Save room for the next stop," warned Sam. "They got brisket braised in beer, the best tater salad you ever ate, and a wheat ale made with apricot purée."

Moments after the server took their order, a different guy came over to their table.

"Don't mean to interrupt, but aren't you Heath Sinclair?"

At the mention of Heath's name, heads turned at the bar.

"Who's asking?"

"Rusty Glisan, brewmaster here. My server's a big fan. He thought he recognized you. He spotted you on the street once in Clarkston.

When he saw the van parked out front, he put two and two together. I got to tell you, your Newberg Neutral kills."

"Thanks. Your porter isn't bad, either."

"You come into the city much?"

"Used to, when I was getting started. Nowadays I'm pretty busy with day-to-day operations."

"This town is like mission central for beer lovers. And we got as many festivals as we have breweries. If you're ever looking for someone to take you around, I'm your man."

"I appreciate it," said Heath, hoisting his mug.

Glisan nodded. "Pleasure's mine."

Red wiped beer foam from her upper lip and giggled. "I didn't know you were famous. I feel like we're your entourage."

"That's just one guy, and he's industry," said Heath humbly.

"Didn't you see those heads turn at the bar when he mentioned your name?"

"There's a lot of us working at Clarkston Craft Ales."

Red turned her attention to Poppy. "So! When's the next public practice session? And can I come and support you?"

"Next Friday night after the consortium closes. Sam will be there, won't you, Sam? And Heath, of course. He's been amazing. I couldn't do this without him."

She sought his eyes, but he averted them, and she knew he was remembering their private session at Sam's bar—and what had almost transpired on his couch.

"Keval will be filming it again. Of course you can come. But not Demi. Everyone is sworn to secrecy so that she doesn't crash it."

"Mum's the word," said Red.

Sam dropped off Red at the café after assuring her he'd use the utmost care taking the new gowns into the consortium, then headed out on Chehalem Creek Road.

After they let Poppy out at her house, Heath climbed into the front with Sam for the short jaunt to his place.

"Pretty productive trip, I'd say," said Sam. "We hit a couple o' great bars, Red got her dresses, and looks like Poppy found herself an apartment."

"Maybe. She didn't put down a deposit."

"No need, yet. It's a brand-new development. There'll still be units available in a month or two, once she finds out for sure if she'll need one."

If. That was the word that was keeping Heath up these nights.

"What do you think about her moving?"

Heath looked out his side window. "I try not to." Every time he did, it tore him up inside.

"That's rough, man. Helping her get what she wants, knowing if she wins, you lose."

"Rub it in, why don't you?" he said miserably.

"Sorry."

They were at his place already.

"Tell me something. You don't think I ought to pull up stakes, move my operation to Portland, do you?"

"Me?" Sam looked genuinely surprised. "Hell no. Not me, man. If you leave town, who am I going to dole out my best under-the-counter hooch to for nothing in return?"

"Nothing? Didn't I pick up your tab today? And who's always the first to get samples of my new releases?"

"Two beers and a pulled pork sandwich. You call that payback? Get outta my van, ya bastard." Grinning from ear to ear, Sam jammed the gearshift into drive to make his point.

With a matching grin, Heath got out and slammed his door.

Friends who could lift you up when you were feeling down weren't easy to come by—let alone leave behind.

He didn't know how Poppy could do it.

That is, unless she didn't really care about whom she was leaving behind.

After all, his own mother hadn't.

Sam honked the horn, and Heath raised a hand in farewell as he trudged toward the house to see how his father fared.

Chapter Twelve

Red kept Poppy occupied over in one of the consortium's comfortable seating nooks while Keval filmed Sam and Heath setting up the blind tasting.

"Did your future boss see the first video when you fell?" asked Red.

Poppy made a face. "Yes, unfortunately."

"Oh no. Did he say anything?"

"What's to say? He just clicked on the link. Letting me know that he had seen it *was* his message."

"Doc," called Sam from over the bar, "would you like some wine?"

Red looked at Poppy for her approval.

"There's plenty to go around. I only need to taste a little from each bottle."

"I'm on my way," called Red, getting up. "You okay here?" she asked Poppy.

"I'm fine! Really. I'm good."

"It won't make you nervous, us watching?"

"I won't be thinking about you. I'll be concentrating on naming the wines."

"Okay then. Good luck."

This time, Sam acted as proctor. He stayed behind the bar while Keval positioned Heath, with the timer, to one side of Poppy and Red on the other for the best camera shot.

"Don't be nervous. You'll do great," said Heath.

"Whenever you're ready," said Keval.

Heath set the timer for twenty-five minutes.

Poppy touched the first glass and the camera started rolling.

"Wine number one is clean, of moderate plus intensity, flavors of apple and honey. Alcohol is high and balanced with a high complexity and a green pepper finish. The bitterness is intense . . . I think this is a two thousand fourteen pinot gris from the Alsace region of France . . ."

She fairly flew through the next four, watching Sam scribble as fast as he could.

"Wine number six is a sweet white wine of moderate plus concentration and caramel color, a perfume of butterscotch and candied orange, a little pineapple. Aged in French oak, this wine is moderately acidic, alcohol is moderate. Final conclusion, this is a dessert wine from Bordeaux, possibly a Sauternes from the Graves region? Stop." She held up her hands. "Time?"

Heath looked up from his phone. "Seventeen minutes. Four minutes faster than last time."

Cheers went up.

"Wait!" She shushed them. "Sam, how many'd I get right?"

There was a pause while he tallied up her score.

"All of them."

This time she was the one shouting, standing on the rail of her bar stool in triumph. "Are you serious? All right?"

With the camera still filming, her friends raised their glasses to her in a toast.

"You did it! You were great!"

"And cut," said Keval, lowering his phone.

A short time later, Poppy's phone blinked.

"It's Cory Anthony! He sent me a private message."

Red leaned over excitedly to spy on her screen. "Oooh! What's it say?"

"Big improvement. Keep at it. See you in a few weeks.'"

When Red led Poppy back over to the lounge area to go over the upcoming fashion show in ever-more-minute detail, Heath found himself wanting to trail after her like some lovesick hound. *They're dresses. How much more can be said?*

But he couldn't walk away from Sam, congratulating him on this latest score of Poppy's.

"*Dayam.* I'm thinking you missed your calling. Should've been a life coach."

"Don't look at me," said Heath, perched sideways on his bar stool watching Poppy's lips move, wishing he could hear her honeyed voice. "That was pure Poppy."

"Guys, guys," Keval tsked. "Don't pretend you don't know what just happened."

Sam and Heath exchanged looks of bewilderment.

"It's easy to see what you did," continued Keval. "You told her what the wines were ahead of time so she'd look good on the video."

"Did not," said Heath, frowning.

"You guys are so sweet," said Keval, thumbing through his phone. "But you could have let me in on your scam. I'm on Team Poppy, too, you know. Did you think I couldn't tell you rigged that whole thing?"

"You're crazy," said Sam.

"Your secret is safe with me. I love Poppy as much as you do. And don't worry. I have Demi's number now, and I'm not going to let her get away with any more of her shenanigans." He lit up suddenly. "Hey, listen to what just showed up. 'Poppy, soon we'll be able to say we knew you when. Come back and see us when you're a famous somm. Love, Sandy & Kyle.'"

"Listen to this one." Sam interrupted Keval to read from his own phone. "It's from Mona Cruz. Remember Mona? Belly-button ring? Jeans so tight you could see the outline of her permit in her back pocket? 'Poppy, so happy you're finally chasing your dreams.'"

But Heath only half heard them. He was back staring at Poppy sitting straight and tall on the couch, happily debating the merits of trumpet skirts versus mermaids versus sheaths.

She looked more confident, more self-assured than ever before.

His knee-jerk reaction was happiness for her and pride in her progress.

But then the dread that had started as a little pain in his heart expanded into a lump that filled his chest.

Poppy was really going to do this. She was really going to grow up and move away, out of his life forever.

Chapter Thirteen

The evening of the fashion show, Heath got himself tangled up in a production issue at the brewery. Between this fall's pumpkin ale—always one of the year's most popular—and their regular beers, tank space was tight, patience running a little thin. And though his team didn't need his two cents, he felt a compulsion to give it to them anyway.

Thing was, he wasn't exactly raring to get to the charity event, to watch Poppy get "hitched" to that self-absorbed pretty boy, Daryl Decaprio—no matter how good the cause might be.

He was pretty sure his staff breathed a sigh of relief to see the sight of the boss's backside finally walking out the door. The kind of people Heath hired didn't need babysitting.

The consortium parking lot was packed when he got there. Clarkston had been buzzing about this event all week. Heath thought it might be big, but not *this* big.

He could hear the music thumping even as he walked through the parking lot.

"Here's your program," yelled a perky usher wearing bright orange lipstick.

"Thought the show would've been half over by now."

"We're getting a late start. You're lucky—you haven't missed a thing."

Lucky. Heath looked down at the folded paper. On the front was a photo of Doofus Decaprio with his arm around a stunning beauty, her face framed in an ivory veil.

So—this is what other people see when they look at Poppy. No wonder that makeup company wanted her to model for them.

As he ogled the photo, he was bumped from behind by the people who were still pouring in.

He stepped out of the surge of bodies and looked around to get the lay of the land. Craning his neck over the heads of what must have been a hundred and fifty women milling around, he recognized the portable stage Sam had told him about. It was shaped like a T, with rows of chairs lined up several columns deep on either side of the long arm.

He decided he would stay right there, hug the farthest wall from the stage and bide his time. Then, as soon as it was over, he'd head over to the bar, make sure there were no problems with the beer service, and then he was out of there.

But no sooner had he found an ideal spot than a long arm waved to him from the front row.

Aw, shit.

Sam had saved him a seat up there.

Heath knew he shouldn't have come. Weddings were nothing but frothy charades, opportunities for women to get dressed up. Fifty percent of marriages ended up splitting, anyway. That included his own parents'.

Heath shook his head, but Sam was insistent.

Cursing under his breath, Heath wove his way through the chattering throng to the prime seats in the house, inside the right angle where the stem of the T met the cross bar.

"I was just going to stand in the back," Heath yelled into Sam's ear.

"No, stay up here, will ya? I need a seat filler for me and Doc. We're going to be hopping up and down, putting out fires. *Capisce?* Be right back."

Sam was gone before Heath could protest again.

He lowered himself to the rented chair sprayed with gold paint and waited for the show to begin.

He felt trapped, surrounded by those women all jabbering at once. Calling across the room, squealing when they spotted a friend they'd probably seen only yesterday. In all that chaos, it was a wonder any one of them could understand a word being said.

Reconciling himself to an hour of pure misery, he sank his chin on his hand and stared straight ahead, wishing he were anywhere but there. It was only going to get worse when he had to witness Poppy paired up with Dickwad Decaprio from his front-row seat.

Ten minutes later, the show still wasn't starting. His restlessness increased. Would Daryl have the audacity to kiss the bride? What if he did? Would anyone but him consider that to be way out of line? Why did he care, anyway? He and Poppy were just friends. The idea that they could ever form a covalent bond was out of the question.

After what seemed like an interminable wait, things finally got under way. The mistress of ceremonies talked briefly about the Brides for a Cause mission, and then down the runway came a parade of hipster guys in beards and bow ties and women in all manner of fancy getups.

Without warning, Red flounced down beside him, out of breath.

"Do you think it's okay?" she asked, dewy with exertion, brow furrowed in concern.

"Best fashion show I've ever seen," he assured her. No need for her to know it was the *only* one he'd seen.

A few minutes later he recognized Junie Hart's mom strutting down the runway wearing a tan-colored dress.

"Ladies," said the MC, "Dr. Jennifer Jepson-Hart, our next model, is wearing the perfect mother-of-the-groom dress. What is it that makes it so perfect, you ask? As all of you former MOGs know, your primary role is to sit down, shut up, and wear beige."

While the women in the crowd exchanged knowing looks and snickered behind their hands, Heath scrubbed a hand across his chin and wished to God he had a beer. He could have made sure his contribution to this affair went smoothly without subjecting himself to this.

Someone came up behind Red and whispered in her ear, and she leapt up and scurried off to solve whatever fresh catastrophe had arisen. A torn seam; a dropped lipstick, most likely.

Moments later, Sam took the seat Red had vacated. He angled his head toward Heath's so he could be heard above the music. "Just got a glimpse of the bride backstage." He made a face and whistled. "Babe City."

Sam had replaced his jeans with trousers. "You clean up good," Heath said, not bothering to conceal his admiration. "First time I've ever seen you in a suit."

"Hands to yourself," muttered Sam, his eyes on the show, grimacing as he ran a finger between his neck and his collar. "I like the ones who sing soprano."

At his cue, Sam leaped easily onto the stage, followed by a half dozen "groomsmen" and Daryl.

Amid much twittering and positioning of cell phone cameras, Heath realized that Sam had been cast in the role of minister—traditionally, the person responsible for saying, "You may now kiss your bride." Frantically, Heath skimmed the program for a hint of the script, but there was no clue as to how far this charade would go.

Even if there was a script, Sam could easily go rogue and improvise. What could anyone do, once it was over? It came down to Sam's whim whether Daryl and Poppy kissed.

He wished to hell the idea didn't bother him so much. He kept telling himself he was being ridiculous. It was just a show. But there was no use denying it—the prospect of Daryl's lips anywhere near Poppy's was driving him up a wall.

The MC said, "And now, ladies and gentlemen, the part you've all been waiting for. Tonight's grand finale features our very best bridal gown, donated to us by the designer herself. That means that unlike many of our other dresses, it has never been worn—not even once." She called out toward the ladies' room that did double duty as a changing area. "Are we ready?"

Following a tense pause, an assistant popped her head out the bathroom door and gave the nod.

"Cue the music!" yelled the MC.

At the first note of the bridal march, the crowd got to its feet and turned as one toward the base of the T.

Heath found himself holding his breath along with everyone else.

And then a vision floated into view. She was wrapped in a column of white that took the shape of her waist, hips and legs, then trumpeted out in a gentle swirl around her ankles.

The angel paused at the foot of the runway to give the audience the full effect, then began to glide forward, leading from the hip.

Left . . . right . . . left . . . right, one foot in front of the other. With every step, the pliable fabric clung to first one thigh and then the other, draping close over her hips and up to her waist where she clutched a tightly bound bouquet. Higher, to where the fabric smoothed out over her breasts, then gathered again at the base of a swan neck.

Heath's hands felt clammy. His heart raced with the obvious

physiological reactions to sex hormones and neurotransmitters gone haywire, activating his stress response.

"She's beautiful, isn't she?"

When did Red come back?

Now the bride was gliding past directly in front of them. With every stride, Heath could almost hear the swoosh of silk over the music.

She looked neither left nor right. A veil covered her face.

But he'd know that scent of orange blossoms and jasmine anywhere.

He was excited, even euphoric. He suddenly couldn't wait to be close to her again in one of their ordinary, innocent get-togethers, to stare into her eyes, indulge himself in her fragrance to his heart's content. Everything about her was just so *easy*. He never felt ill at ease around *her*.

Then she was past him, and he realized he was standing there like a statue amidst hoots and catcalls and a smattering of applause. He tried to swallow, but the sides of his throat stuck together. His adrenaline and cortisol levels must be off the charts.

In the center of the stage, the woman in white pivoted to face the audience.

The music stopped.

Daryl reached over and lifted her veil, and Heath gasped. *That bone structure . . .* though he'd seen it a thousand times before, somehow he'd never appreciated it.

Sam's mouth was moving as he read from an open book he held before him. There was a terse exchange between Daryl and Poppy. Sam uttered some directive, and then Daryl leaned in and bussed Poppy's cheek, and the crowd erupted into fresh cheers, while Heath took in the scene like watching his future unfolding in slow motion. Dopey Decaprio's kiss didn't matter at all. What mattered was that suddenly, all the puzzle pieces in Heath's broken life came together as he recognized the only thing that could make him whole again.

Poppy.

He drove home in a daze. Halfway there, it occurred to him: he never did check on the beer.

Chapter Fourteen

"Are you kidding me?"

Sam stood inside the threshold of Heath's new house with his hands propped casually on his hips. "*How* many people live here?" he asked with his typical sarcasm.

His words echoed throughout the cavernous interior. The house was still settling into its site, just as Heath was still settling within its walls. He still got occasional whiffs of freshly stained wood.

Heath jammed his hands into the pockets of his jeans and rocked back and forth on his soles. "Me."

Guinness, sitting patiently beside the console that held the dog biscuits, barked.

"And these guys," he added, on his way to get Guinness his bone.

Outside a sliding door, Amber clamored for attention, and Heath let her in while Sam strolled around the sparely furnished great room.

From its inception, Heath intended that this place was going to be clean and sleek, not cluttered, like his old house.

Sam whistled. "All this empty space. How do you intend to spend your time here all by yourself?"

Heath shrugged. "Maybe do some gardening." He loved plants almost as much as he loved animals.

Sam made a face. "Gardening."

"Yeah. Gardening." Who cared what Sam thought? He was still waiting for Sam to tell him why he had shown up at his place, unannounced.

"What, get one of those little gnomes, set it out in the front yard?"

"Maybe."

"What about people?"

"What about them?"

"Don't you want to get hitched someday? Have a couple o' little beer nuts?" asked Sam, strolling over to the picture window that looked down through the woods to the creek. "Shame not to share this."

Heath's mind was still reeling from the fashion show. It was one thing to see Poppy all glammed up on the stage in that fantasy setting, another to transfer that fantasy to reality.

Let someone else into my carefully crafted world, put everything on the line, only to be abandoned all over again?

"I've got my dad next door. The guys at work. Rory. Keval. You."

"I'm not talking about us assjacks. You know what I mean. A woman. Nothing like a woman to make a man feel alive."

Whispered offers of favors . . . perfunctory actions between unfamiliar sheets. All his past encounters with women flew into Heath's memory. "I've had my share."

He wasn't a robot.

"Just not here," quipped Sam, reading between the lines.

Sam was right, as usual. Heath had never brought a woman here. This house was sacred space. It had never been designed with casual hookups in mind.

Damn that Sam. Someday, he was going to get to the bottom of that spy rumor.

"Like I said, I'm fine the way things are. I don't need anyone."

"Au contraire, amigo. If nothing else, you could use someone to bounce wardrobe ideas off," said Sam, eyeballing Heath's T-shirt.

"What?" Heath asked, looking down at the silk-screened picture of Bill Nye the Science Guy emblazoned on his chest. "This is my best shirt."

"Forget it. So how do you handle a trusted old friend who happens to have a hot body?"

Heath blinked. "That doesn't compute."

Ugh. Maybe he *was* a robot.

"Seriously, man. What's Poppy think of this Shangri-La?"

There was a pause while Heath tried to think of something to say that wouldn't have Sam calling him the biggest wuss he'd ever met.

"Don't tell me. She hasn't seen it." Sam looked at him askance. "You've gotta be kidding. You've got this showplace and a woman like Poppy Springer close enough to nab with a shepherd's crook, and you haven't put two and two together yet? What are you waiting for? An engraved invitation?"

Heath looked away. They had a lot of shared past to overcome. Maybe *too* much.

"It's not like that with me and Poppy."

"Are you blind, man? Do you not see the way she looks at you?"

His head jerked up. True, she had gotten a little carried away that night at the consortium. But she said it was because she was psyched about acing the blind tasting. Heath had taken her at face value.

"Poppy doesn't want to live in Clarkston anymore. She wants adventure and prestige."

"Poppy wants to feel good about herself. That's what she wants. All anyone wants. I got news for you, man. There's more than one path to nirvana."

"She asked for my help."

"You can help her without reading her the damn road map to the fastest route out of town."

Sam tried out the black tufted leather couch, crossing his legs, extending one arm along its back. "Try showing her what's right next door.

"Hey, cat," he said, ruffling Vienna's head.

Mrrrw. Vienna leaped down off the couch and stalked away haughtily, tail held high.

Sam might be a lot of things, but he didn't know how to handle a cat—patiently, letting *her* come to *you.*

"Far be it from me to stick my nose in another man's business, but if I were in your boots, you know what I'd do?" Before Heath could reply, Sam charged ahead. "Invite her over here. Show her there's more to this town than her bedroom in her parents' house and her waitress job."

"That sounds manipulative to me. Besides, I like—"

"Yeah, yeah. You're subtle. You like your privacy. Blah blah blah. But sometimes you got to take a risk, man. Give up something in the short run to get what you want in the long haul. Hell, you know what I'm talking about. You're a businessman. You need to step out of your comfort zone to get ahead. Never know what you might find."

Heath had had enough of Sam's unsolicited advice. "What did you ever risk? Seems like everything fell into your lap as soon as you got back from the service." Sam had a golden-boy aura about him that made it seem as though he'd never struggled for anything.

A shadow crossed Sam's face. "Things aren't always what they seem." He looked at his watch. "Shit. I got a meeting in ten." Hopping to his feet, he said, "Thanks for the tour. Props on this place. You did a bang-up job."

He gave Heath's shoulder a fraternal squeeze on their way out to his logo-splashed van.

But instead of climbing into the driver's seat, Sam reached into the back and came out with a half case of wine and deposited it in Heath's arms.

"What's this?"

"Partials left over from Poppy's practice sessions. Bought and paid for. Be a shame to let good wine go to waste. Besides, with all the wine rolling into my place on a daily, I don't have much extra storage space. But you do."

"Why don't you take it to her yourself? It's only a minute out of your way."

Sam folded his arms against the late October chill, crossed one leg over the other and relaxed against the side of his van. "I could do that," he said with a look laden with meaning. "Or you could ask her to drop by, get it herself."

A legitimate reason to invite Poppy over lent Sam's advice added weight.

Memories came to Heath unbidden: Poppy's body arching beneath his on Sam's red couch that night when they had the whole consortium to themselves, her eager, grasping hands urging him ever closer.

But as she said, she was just jacked up about having done well on her tasting. The real Poppy was a sweet girl next door who had a nice family, a chocolate Lab, and a hankering to leave town. A fully rounded person, not one of those craft beer groupies, out to etch another notch on her tulip glass.

Sam ducked into the driver's seat, punched the ignition button, and grabbed the interior door handle, but Heath's hand blocked it from closing.

"You're pretty free with the relationship advice, seeing's how you don't have a woman, either."

To Heath's surprise, Sam threw back his head, opened wide, and laughed, the heartening sound ringing out in the quiet woods. "When we're through with you, we'll get me one, too." With that, he gunned the engine.

Heath grinned in spite of himself as he watched his friend's van circle through his driveway and pull out onto Chehalem Creek Road toward town.

Sam's right, he thought, walking back to the house.

But Heath wasn't Sam, suave and confident and people-savvy. His style was more cautious and tentative. He had to wait until the time felt right.

Besides, this autumn he had the luxury of seeing Poppy whenever he wanted. It was almost too easy. He had her schedule memorized. All he had to do was stop in the café when he knew she would be working—which he did, nearly every day.

October slipped by. Heath closed up the tree house for the winter. He and Poppy went on as if that night at the consortium had never happened.

Every so often they got together with their group for a movie or drinks.

In early November, Poppy invited him to her place to help her go over potential test questions at her kitchen table, while in the living room her parents watched TV.

The next time he came over, her parents were out somewhere. By now, sitting next to Poppy with that scent wafting around him and nobody else around was making him go crazy with desire. Halfway through their session he brushed his foot against hers under the table, and when she looked up in surprise, his eyes delved into hers.

"How about some ice cream?" Poppy jumped up and hid her blush behind the open freezer door.

Without thinking twice, Heath got up, walked over to her like an automaton, took the ice cream carton out of her hand and set it on the counter. "I don't want ice cream." He folded her in his arms and kissed her breathless. "I want this," he murmured, sliding his hand under her shirt in the back.

His surprise attack seemed to be working. She was every bit as ardent as he, her hands raking over his body, wrinkling his T-shirt, pressing his hips into hers.

But after a minute she pulled back. "What are we doing?" she gasped, red-faced and wet-lipped, her hair tumbling over her forehead where he'd run his hands through it, hiding half her face.

"We're making out."

"No! I mean, what are we *doing* doing?"

"Uh, like I said . . ."

"Heath," she said, turning her back on him, planting her palms on the counter, trying to catch her breath.

"We agreed we can't do this. It's not good. Not for me, and certainly not for you."

Then the sound of her parents' tires crunching up the gravel driveway had them hurriedly wiping their mouths and straightening their clothes and Poppy furtively scooping an enormous bowl of ice cream for Heath, which he couldn't think of eating. And once again, things went back to the way they'd been before they reached puberty.

Mid-November, her mom had him over for spaghetti. Heath's dad was invited, too, but of course, he didn't go.

Thanksgiving weekend, Poppy set up another table service get-together at the consortium. This time, there were no catastrophes.

In all that time, Sam's suggestion was never far from Heath's mind. He knew time was running out. Soon he would go from seeing Poppy whenever he wanted, to who knew how often.

When December came, he started getting anxious. He tried dropping a few broad hints about coming over to his place, but she didn't take the bait.

Once, he came this close to actually inviting her over, but he remembered her terms, and he wasn't at all sure he could trust himself if she did. There wasn't much time left until her exam. He didn't want to rock the boat.

But a few days later, the temptation became too much. He decided he would ask her in for one final study session. It would be just like when they were kids and he tutored her at the café while eating fries and drinking lemonade. Only this time, he'd pick up some grown-up food: an assortment of good cheese and some artisanal bread. Nothing over the top. He didn't want to look too obvious.

The day before her test, Heath paced the hallway, practicing the script he'd carefully composed to Guinness and Amber until they got bored and trotted away in search of something more interesting.

Then he took a deep breath and called Poppy up.

Chapter Fifteen

"It's me."

"I know." Poppy grinned to herself. Heath's name had been on her favorites list since her very first phone. Yet, in all those years, she could count on one hand the number of times he'd called her.

"Everything okay?"

"Yeah. I just . . ."

"Yes?" She lowered the list of top-rated wines she was trying to commit to memory and flounced back into the pink bed pillows stacked against her headboard. Just yesterday, she'd overheard some visiting hopheads down at the café bragging about having spotted the reclusive Heath Sinclair walking down Main Street "just like a regular person." If they only knew how human he was, how flawed. How *dear.*

"Um, yeah, I was wondering . . ." He coughed. "'Scuse me. What you are doing?"

"Right now?" She looked past the doodles she'd scribbled all over her study guide to help lodge the vocabulary in her mind, to the papers scattered across her flowered comforter. There was still so much to learn, and only hours left before her test.

But her head was filled to bursting with wine names, descriptors, vintages. She was tired of studying. Impulsively, she balled up her paper and threw it across the room.

"Nothing."

"Would you like to, uh, come over here, to my place?"

"The tree house? Sorry. Too cold for me. It's supposed to get below freezing tonight. Might even snow."

"Not the tree house. The house. The real house."

Concern gripped her. Hardly anyone had seen the inside of Heath's new place. Everyone had been patiently biding their time until he felt comfortable extending an invitation. "Is something wrong?"

"No. Nothing's wrong."

It occurred to her that maybe he'd invited others over, too. "Is it just going to be us?"

There was an uncertain pause. "Yeah," he said, his voice cracking. He cleared his throat. "Yeah. Just us."

She bit her lip. They'd managed to quell their—whatever it was that they had—for a while, until he had kissed her in her mother's kitchen. Since then, Poppy had gotten flustered and out of breath every time he walked into the café. Being all alone with him in that big house in the woods was way too risky.

"I need to be up bright and early tomorrow morning to drive to Portland," she said, fanning her face.

"I just thought . . . if there're still some things you're struggling with . . . I could quiz you one last time."

Darn it, Heath, just stop. Don't you see? It's you who's going to get hurt when I leave.

"Poppy, I—"

She clutched the phone, waiting with bated breath for his next words.

"I need to see you. Just for a little while."

Just like that. No practical reason, not even a made-up excuse. She knew how hard that was for Heath. How could she say no?

"Okay. But I can't stay long."

Fifteen minutes later, Poppy raised her fist to knock on Heath's door, but he opened it before she made contact.

"Brrr!" She strode in without waiting to be asked.

She did a double take. He looked different. He'd got his hair cut, and in place of his usual geeky tee, he had on a woven shirt, sleeves stylishly turned up, top three buttons left undone.

"Nice shirt."

"You like it?" he asked, looking down at himself self-consciously.

But while he closed the door against the cold, she was already exploring.

"You walked," she heard him say from behind her.

"I've been studying for hours. I needed some fresh air. It's starting to sn—oh my God." She stopped and stared slack-jawed at the living room wrapped in glass, anchored with a black leather sectional atop a subtly patterned Oriental rug. Outside, along multitiered rooflines, yellow lights lit up the cobalt evening sky and made the slowly falling snowflakes twinkle.

Mesmerized, Poppy stepped into the clean, modern space.

"Heath," she breathed, "this is amazing. You really designed this yourself?"

"I had some ideas. The architect drew up the blueprint."

She tossed her bag on the ottoman and slipped out of her coat, not sure what to do with it.

"I'll take that."

After Heath rushed to take her coat and disappeared with it, she headed to the crackling fire to warm her chilled hands.

He was back in no time. "I wanted the fireplace to be double sided so you could enjoy it both in here and outside on the terrace."

"Like the bed in your tree house."

"Exactly."

She never should have mentioned the word "bed." She dragged her eyes away from her surroundings back to him. "I'm speechless."

"Make a note. First time Poppy Springer was ever at a loss for words."

"Ha." She poked him good-naturedly in the side, and instantly, the details of her hands splayed across his back and sides and chest that night at the consortium came back to her. Then and now, he was like a rock.

Something stirred in her lower belly.

"Come on. I'll show you the kitchen."

Behind his back, she couldn't help but sneak a peek at where his plaid shirt disappeared into his jeans.

His house wasn't the only thing that was well-built.

Unlike in most kitchens, no appliances lined the perimeter. Instead, the sinks and a cooktop were set into two long islands, one stainless steel and the other rough-hewn wood topped with butcher block.

Air plants in glass bubbles suspended over the islands at varying heights softened the masculine edges of the room.

Poppy gravitated toward the island with a half dozen wine bottles sitting on it.

She picked up one and looked at the label. "Pinot gris." Then an-other. "Saint-Émilion, two thousand ten. Are these—?" She looked at him with a question in her eyes.

Heath got two glasses from a cupboard flush with the wall. "Your leftovers. Sam brought them here."

Playfully, she turned down her lip. "You invited Sam here before me?"

"No." He hurried to console her.

"That's okay. You're allowed to invite anyone here you want, whenever you want. I was just . . . a little jealous."

"You were?"

Yes, she was. That he was surprised only endeared him to her all the more. If she'd been wondering how well she'd managed to hide her secret attraction these past weeks, now she knew.

She took a mental step back, trying to examine Heath objectively, as if she hadn't grown up with him, didn't know all of his issues by heart. Physically, he was a nicely proportioned guy. Kind of quiet, but bathed regularly. Good job, kind to animals. What wasn't to like?

But she had to tread carefully. The problem was, she *couldn't* be objective for long. She knew him too well—and all that he'd been through. She was leaving soon, and the last thing she wanted was to subject him to more rejection.

"Sam stopped by to see the house on his own."

"That's Sam for you." She chuckled. "Wouldn't let a little thing like an invitation keep him away."

"He had the wine in his van. He asked me to give it to you."

"He wanted to save himself an extra stop," she deduced, testing the feel of a silk drapery between her fingers. "If I'd known that's why you asked me over, I'd have driven."

"That's one reason."

She turned and faced him full on. "What's the other one?" she asked, knowing she was only inviting trouble.

"Time's running out. I wanted you to see it before . . ." He turned and picked up a clean dish towel to wipe at an imaginary smudge on a glass. "You know."

He couldn't even say the *word* "leave." Her heart squeezed a lit-tle more.

"Well," she smiled wistfully, "I'm glad you did."

Heath picked up a bottle. "Which one do you want?"

"The zin will do."

They carried their glasses into the living room. Poppy curled up at one end while Heath sat stiffly at the other.

She sipped her wine. "Mm. This is very relaxing."

"So. You ready for this?"

Her head whipped around.

"I didn't mean *this*. I meant, you know, *tomorrow*."

"As ready as I can be. You've already helped me so much. We don't have to do any more. Studying, that is. But just in case, I brought some stuff we haven't gone over before."

"I'll take a look."

She pulled her folders from her bag and handed them to him, chuckling lightly. "It's okay to scootch closer."

He inched closer, but not much.

She cradled her glass in her lap. "Mix up the order a bit, if you wouldn't mind."

"Okay," he said, back in his element now that they had something concrete with which to occupy themselves. "Here we go. Which New Zealander sold his namesake sauvignon blanc label in two thousand three and started the organic brand called Loveblock?"

"Kim Crawford."

"Good.

"In eighteen fifty-five, the merchants of Bordeaux chose sixty-one prime estates and put them into five classes. In what area of France were these estates located?"

"The Médoc."

"Next, what is the most distinctive characteristic of German wines?"

"High acidity."

"Three for three. But these are just one-word answers. What about your essay questions?"

"There're some on the back. I'm going to get a tad more wine. There wasn't much left in that first bottle. And then I have to go. You?"

He drained his glass and held it out to her. "Sure."

"Here's a tough one for you," said Heath when she returned. "Describe the Italian technique used to make amarone."

She tucked a leg under her and pictured the map of Italy. "Amarone is made in Verona from only the 'ears,' the grapes protruding outside the cluster that get the most sun. The process is called recioto."

He nodded, impressed. "You've been hard at it."

"I have to know the material better than anyone else because it takes me longer to write down my answers. Once that clock starts ticking, I can't take precious time to figure things out."

"Okay. No more Mr. Nice Guy. Time to go full on."

Poppy raised her glass. "Bring it."

"Define meritage and describe how it is made."

She was ready for this one. "Meritage is a blend of cabernet sauvignon, merlot, cabernet franc, malbec, and . . ." She scowled. At least, she thought she was ready. "What's that other one?"

"Mm-mm. No helping this time."

"Petit verdot."

He nodded.

"You have to keep each varietal separate during vinification and aging. Then you decide how much of each to blend before you bottle it."

Too soon, their glasses were empty again.

"I feel like having another, if that's okay with you."

"Of course. What's mine is yours."

"I know you said you have to go, so I'm not pressuring you, but I wouldn't be polite if I didn't offer . . ."

She hesitated. She was so done with months of studying. Now it was almost over. No more holing up in her parents' house every evening. No more schlepping coffee to unappreciative diners. No more mopping up dried egg yolk from under high chairs. She couldn't wait. "Sure! Why not? I'm in the mood to celebrate."

While fat flakes of snow fell outside, they worked their way through page after page of her notes in front of the fireplace.

And whenever their glasses were empty, one of them would get up and refill them.

"Name five historic types of decanters," said Heath as Poppy returned with yet another round.

"Um, lemme see." She fell onto her back on the couch, her head landing on Heath's lap, and counted on her fingers. "There's cruciform . . . globe and something . . ."

"Shaft," said Heath. "It says here, shaft and globe."

"Shaft and globe, um, mallet? Is mallet one?"

"Mallet." He nodded.

"Yay! Mallet! High five!"

They took aim—and missed.

Poppy collapsed into gales of laughter. "We're some pair, you and me! We can't even manage a high five!"

With some effort she drew herself back to sitting, holding her head. "Ohhh. My brain is drained." She gulped yet more wine. "And look—my glass is, too!" She rose, giggling when the room wobbled. "You wan' some more?"

Heath was on his feet, reaching out to steady her, but the ottoman caught the back of her knees and her bottom plopped onto it.

"Whoa!" She laughed.

"Better let me walk you home," said Heath.

"Not now. I'm having too much fun."

Moments later he called from the kitchen, "The wine's all gone."

"No way!" Poppy yelled, heading out to the kitchen to see for herself.

She shut one eye and peered inside bottle after bottle. Then she turned them upside down and shook them over her glass, but only a few, sad drops fell out.

"Oh, pooh!"

"We went through six bottles."

"But some of them only had a little itty bit in them," she said, squinting between her thumb and index finger.

He grinned lazily and pulled her toward him. "How much did they have?"

"A little itty—" She pouted. "You're making fun of me."

Heath slid his arms around her waist and pulled her hips into his.

"Never," he growled, gazing into her eyes. "I would never, ever make fun of you. Y'know why?"

Heath's body felt firm against hers. His arms were warm and protective against the cold black winter night, visible from every angle through all that glass.

"You should drink wine more often," she said. "This is nice."

She tried to focus up into his half-closed eyes. "What was that you were starting to say a minute ago? Oh yeah. You said you would never make fun of me. Why is that?"

"Because I—"

She seemed to have lost her reserve, somewhere along the way. She bit her lower lip and batted her eyes, flirting shamelessly.

"Because you what?"

"Because you're . . ."

He sat down his glass on the island, then took hers from her hand and did the same.

Then he cradled her face.

"What? What am I to you, Heath Sinclair?" she urged. "Tell me."

The firelight flickered gold in his hazel eyes. His thumb stroked the line of her jaw, and she closed her eyes and leaned into the feeling.

The stroking stopped. Disappointed, she opened her eyes to see that for once, the usual aloofness was nowhere to be found. In its place was something fathomless. Something powerful.

He pressed his forehead to hers.

His hesitancy was driving her crazy. Couldn't he tell she wanted him? Hadn't her brazen actions said that loud and clear?

"Come with me."

"Of course," she hiccupped happily. "Lead the way."

Poppy let herself be led out of the kitchen, down a long hallway.

"How come you built a house that's all windows? Thought you liked privacy."

"There's nothing outside. No one can see us but the deer."

They stumbled into a square room where the outline of a king-sized bed was faintly visible in the glow from the lights strung along the eaves.

They were kissing before they made it to the mattress, the sounds of mouth on wet mouth and heavy breathing amplified in the hushed silence of the empty house, the snowy night.

A dark shape tried to sneak in behind them.

"Guinness. Out," said Heath, shutting the door behind him with his foot.

Finally, finally, *finally!* Poppy thought.

Dizzy with the onslaught, Poppy could barely suppress her smile despite her mouth being captive to his never-ending kisses. She had wanted this. Wanted it more than she knew.

* * *

Heath's hands slid under her sweater, up and over her head. She fumbled with the buttons on his crisp new shirt. Impatiently, he took over and soon cast it aside.

In the half darkness, he could see the gentle curves where her perfectly formed breasts disappeared into the slippery fabric of her bra. They looked deliciously new and yet familiar, and for the very first time, he acknowledged foggy teenage memories of watching them blossom over summers at the Clarkston Pool.

With the back of a finger he traced a line down to her navel. The bedroom wasn't as warm as the living room, and she shivered in the cool air, or at his touch, or both.

Already aroused, he slipped his finger into her stretchy waistband.

She moaned and raised one leg, wrapping it around his waist.

He planted a hand on that knee and pushed it back down. "You don't need these," he said, shoving his hands into her pants and slipping them off, then reaching behind her knee to pull it firmly back into position.

It wasn't enough. Hungrily, he hoisted her rear end up and she instinctively wrapped her other leg around him. But their coordination was compromised, and he tumbled backward onto the bed with her straddling him, her hair falling around his face like a curtain.

The cloud of her scent surrounding him was more intoxicating than the wine. Adrenaline flooded his system. His jeans suddenly felt as constricting as a prison. He shoved her hips up onto his waist and struggled to break free of them while the warm silk of her panties and the weight of what was in them rocked against his abs.

She's the girl next door, for Chrissake. How could he want to ravish her like he did?

But he did. Oh, he so did.

Eagerly he reached up to palm her breasts. She bent forward, aiming one at his mouth, and whimpered when he opened his mouth and sucked on the silky fabric, so thin he wondered what frivolous purpose it served.

"Oh, Heath."

At the sound of his name on her breath, something primal came over him. He flipped her over onto her back.

* * *

Poppy opened her eyes to Heath kneeling between her legs. One hand was planted on either side of her head. His eyes were doing a slow tour of her body. When they returned to hers, the tiny line between his brows was furrowed with restrained passion.

Words weren't Heath's forté. But tonight, words were superfluous. She could read his eyes, his body language. They were at a tipping point, and he was waiting for a sign.

"Forget the past, and the future," she said. "Tonight is ours."

In answer, he kissed her lips, first gently, then building in intensity.

His mouth forged a new frontier, down her neck to previously forbidden territories and up again, his hands everywhere, tangling in her hair, now gripping a calf, now lifting her hips, shoving a pillow beneath them, angling her to his advantage, and the next time he reached between her legs, the anticipation alone sent her over the edge.

Above all, Heath was a giving man. He gave until she begged him to stop, and then he gave some more.

Only then did he center her on the pillow to take his own satisfaction, and Poppy felt a rush of feminine euphoria when he finally drove into her, filling her. She moved with him until they reached a triumphant peak, Heath's hoarse cry of release in her ear proof of the joy he took in her.

When it was over, he collapsed onto his back.

"It's not fair," she panted.

His head lolled toward hers, looking suddenly worried. "What's not fair?" Lazily, he reached beneath the sheets, brushing his fingers across her most sensitive spot as lightly as a butterfly's wing. "Are you . . . didn't you . . . ?"

She twitched and sucked in a shattered breath. "So many times. It's not that. What I meant was, it's not fair that women have two kinds of pleasure and men only have one."

He rolled onto his back again and threw an arm over his head. "Ah. Good to know our, uh, bonding mechanism works."

A laugh burst from her throat. "Oh, it works."

He leaned over a third time and kissed her swollen lips, then fell back and closed his eyes.

In no time, his breath evened into the slow rhythm of sleep.

Tucked away in the woods above the creek, she had never felt so satisfied . . . so serene . . . so protected. Like they were in their own, safe world.

She curled into Heath's side and, for a moment, watched the snow fall and listened to the steady heartbeat of this man she'd known since he was a child, then she closed her eyes and slept.

Chapter Sixteen

Poppy threw back the covers in a panic.

The room, attractive as it was with its soft gray upholstery in the pale morning light, was strange to her.

Outside the wall of glass across from the bed, a light blanket of snow coated the soft firs, the naked maple and oak branches.

What time is it?

She felt for her phone.

Seven fifteen!

Heath lay on his stomach, his face half-buried in his pillow. Now she knew a whole different side of him—and he, of her.

Passionate scenes came back to her like fast-forwarding through a movie. Never again would she see a boy when she looked at him. He was all man.

She swept her clothes up from the carpet, revealing a threadbare stuffed dog lying beneath them. Wasting valuable seconds, she bent and picked it up, passing a fingertip over its sole button eye. It was very old. It must have been perched on Heath's bed before they wrecked it in their—what had he called it? Bonding mechanism?

Smiling softly with the memory, she brought the well-loved toy to her nose. The green woods down by Chehalem Creek immediately sprang to mind, followed by a trace of Heath's worn leather jacket with a whiff of the same laundry soap used on his sheets.

Nostalgia filled her to bursting. She pressed the dog to her heart and looked back at Heath's sleeping face.

Years of fond memories flashed through her mind.

She stood on the threshold of a brand-new life. If she was successful, it would mean walking away from all of this.

Stealing was wrong. That lesson had been learned early, the couple of times customers had ducked out on their bills at the café, to her parents' dismay.

Before her better judgment kicked in she bundled Heath's special dog into her balled-up clothes and tiptoed down the stairs.

She was exiting the powder room when Heath appeared at the top of the steps.

She jumped. "Morning!" she called, trying to sound as normal as possible, although nothing about this morning was normal.

"Where are you going?"

"I've got at least an hour's drive ahead of me." She grabbed her bag from the ottoman, then her eyes scanned the living room. "Where's my coat?"

His hand was on her arm before she realized he had descended the stairs. "You're still going?"

The little vertical lines between his brows were deeper than ever.

"Why wouldn't I be? This is what I've been working so hard for for the past three months."

Spying her coat on a hook by the back door, she strode over and snatched it herself while his hand drifted in slow motion back down to his side. "But—what about last night?"

"Last night was amazing." She bussed his slack lips as she worked her arms into her coat sleeves and headed for the door. "I'll never forget it. I'll call you," she said, fumbling with the latch.

"But—can't I just tell you something?"

Despite her urgency, she turned back around.

He'd known her all his life. He'd picked now to open up? *Today?*

"I have an idea."

The sight of him standing in his doorway bare-chested, a trail of tawny curls disappearing into pajama bottoms held up by a flimsy drawstring, suddenly made her want to chuck the whole sommelier idea. Run back into his arms and spend the day making love all over again.

"An idea?"

"For my business."

Her head spun. If his so-called idea had had anything at all to do with feelings, with the two of them, that was one thing. But business?

"I've decided to open a bar out front of my brewery. Like a tasting room for wine, but for beer."

She angled toward the door. "Heath, I—"

"No, wait." He closed the distance between them. "I've been giving it a lot of thought. Brewpubs as a main place of sales for breweries are way up. They're a trending business model, and my brewery's in the perfect spot, right along the main road into town where all the tourists will be sure to see it. Financing's not a problem. Neither is selling the idea to my team. They've been on me to do this for a while. So has Sam, and you know how astute he is . . ."

She was pretty sure she'd just witnessed the longest monologue of Heath's life. That novelty was the only thing still keeping her there.

"You want to open a bar. That's great. Why are you telling me this? Why now?"

He reached for her hand with both of his.

"I need you, Poppy."

Her heart played a cruel game of tug-of-war with her head.

"What craft beer drinkers want is to rub shoulders with the brewer and his team. Interact, ask questions."

"I still don—"

"I can't do it alone. I need your help, just like I always have. Like the time you dragged me to Sam's birthday party, and the way you always made me go to the Clarkston Splash and the post–Memorial Day Hike. If not for you, I wouldn't have half the friends I have now."

"But I know next to nothing about beer."

"I'll teach you everything you need to know. If a customer's question stumps you, I'll be right there to answer it. What can't be taught is how to be naturally outgoing, like you are. I need a born front-of-the-house person. I need you by my side."

She turned to face him head-on.

"Let me get this straight. You need me . . . to *work* for you?"

He shook his head vigorously. "Not as an employee. As a partner. In exchange for your help, I'll give you a share in the business."

She threw up her hands, turned, and flounced down the driveway.

"Wait! Aren't you even going to think about it?"

"Your timing's a little off," she hollered over her shoulder. *And to think I felt guilty about leaving him!* He was completely, utterly clueless.

"Is it the money? Granted, you won't make as much as you could working for Anthony. At least, not at first."

For the very last time, she marched back to him. "You think this is about money? Money has nothing to do with it. It's my self-worth that's on the line. I studied hard for this test, and I'm not going to blow it for some bar that you just conjured up out of thin air!"

She shook her head, leaving him standing there with a desolate look on his face.

She heard the scrape of car keys across wood followed by the slap of bare feet on concrete.

"At least let me give you a ride," he pleaded.

"I'll walk," she called over her shoulder.

The snow was already melting as she made tracks back to her house. All she had time to do was change and jump into her car.

Feelings! She should have known. Despite last night, Heath was as out of touch with his feelings as ever.

Good luck with your stupid brewpub.

She couldn't be late for that test. How could she have drunk so much last night when she knew how important today was?

Out of habit, she checked her phone as she walked. There was a message from her mom, left around midnight. "You're probably still at Heath's, but could you please give me a call to let me know you weren't kidnapped?"

Poppy slipped her phone back into her bag. She couldn't wait until she didn't have to check in with Mom and Pop anymore.

And yet . . . More scenes from last night tormented her. For someone so insensitive in the living room, he sure made up for it in bed.

Firmly, she pushed Heath out of her mind and concentrated hard on grape varieties, estates, processes, and characteristics. But everything swam together.

She sucked in cleansing breaths of frosty morning air. But the rawness between her legs with every step was a nagging reminder of her error in judgment. She should never have gone over there.

She couldn't think about that right now. She had a test to pass.

Heath watched Poppy scurry down his driveway, already lost in her phone.

How could she let the outside world back in so quickly? Last night had meant everything to him. He'd be lost in the memory for days.

He had been so happy when he woke up this morning with her next to him in his bed. What had gone wrong?

The concept of pairing up with Poppy for the bar was like a gift, given to him as he lay in that groggy onset of wakefulness.

Granted, building a brewpub would be a huge commitment. He'd have to put himself out there with the public on a regular basis. Push past his boundaries.

But with her by his side, there was nothing he couldn't do. And then, just in time for the reunion, she wouldn't be the yearbook's same Poppy-from-the-café. Which meant she wouldn't feel like she had to move away anymore.

It was the ideal solution to all their problems.

Except that she hadn't quite seen it that way.

He was faintly aware of Guinness begging for a bone, Vienna winding around his ankles, wanting fed, and Amber wagging at door, waiting to be let out.

He'd let his guard down last night. Let Poppy in. Showed her a side of himself he'd never shown another woman. He'd thought it had meant as much to her as it did to him.

His eye landed on her wineglass sitting on the counter, a dime-sized purple stain in the center. He snatched it and hurled it against the wall.

Guinness skittered sideways at the sound of shattering glass, losing traction on the slippery tile, and then cowered in a corner.

Poor Amber had disappeared, out of sight. Heath scrubbed a hand through his hair and paced the cold tiles, glimpsing from the corner of his eye the tip of Vienna's tail disappearing at the top of the stairs.

What is it about me that makes people leave?

He crouched next to Guinness, comforting him with a soft word and a gentle hand, a tear stuck in his eye.

At least he had his animals. They were the only ones who loved him unconditionally.

Then he went to sweep up the broken glass.

Chapter Seventeen

Outside the ballroom door of the big hotel where the test was being held, Poppy paused to catch her breath and tuck an errant wisp of hair into her ponytail.

This is it.

She took a deep breath and opened the door.

Inside, the other candidates milled about, waiting for the service part of the test to begin. Every one of them appeared to be smarter than she was. More professional, more confident. She'd bet her last dime none of *them* had been dumb enough to spend last night in a whirlwind of booze and sex.

But there was no time to dwell on her mistake. Moments later, she was pinning on her name tag and her group was being ushered into an inner waiting room where a proctor gave them instructions on how to proceed.

An hour later, the service phase of the test was finished.

She hadn't dropped a tray, broken a glass, or put out any eyes with a champagne cork, but when asked which region of Spain sherry was from, she had drawn a complete blank. Of course, now that the test was over she remembered that it was Jerez.

And when trying to do an even pour of Bordeaux, she had come up short on the fourth and tried to compensate by emptying the bottle to the last drop, which meant some sediment had gone into the glass. Maybe not such a big deal in real life, but the sharp-eyed judge had seen it and marked something on his grading sheet.

And service was supposed to be her strength.

Well. Nothing she could do about it now.

Next came the blind tasting.

Thanks to her good friends—especially Heath—giving up their time and energy to help her practice, she felt certain she'd correctly identified at least four of the wines. She was reasonably sure of the fifth and had taken a random stab at the sixth.

She'd done a decent job of compartmentalizing her thoughts until now, the written part, when she needed to be the most clear-headed. But she couldn't stop thinking about last night.

And once she was seated at a long table with her test paper in front of her, every question brought to mind Heath's face, the sound of his voice, their shared laughter as they wrestled with French place names. That's when it occurred to her: Everything she knew about wine to this point was inextricably intertwined with him.

By four p.m., it was all over. The judges shook her hand and said she should expect to hear something within a day or two.

She drove back to Clarkston, limp with exhaustion. Her limbs ached, her head throbbed.

In the past twenty-four hours, she had given all she had to give.

All day long, Heath thought about Poppy and her test.

He wouldn't interrupt her, and yet he had so much more to say to her. To ask her.

How the test had gone, of course. But that wasn't all.

In the hours after she left his house, a sickening realization washed over him.

Did she think he'd tried to sabotage her?

Had he? Did he get her drunk last night so she'd flunk her test?

No way, nohow. He would never intentionally set her up to fail, even if it benefited him.

But what if that was how it turned out? If she failed because she wasn't at her best, who would blame her if she thought him the worst kind of creep?

Estimating that the test wouldn't go later than five o'clock, he counted down the minutes, and then, at five sharp, punched in her number.

Would she even pick up, after this morning's awkwardness?

After what he'd done, would she ever speak to him again?

With every unanswered ring, his heart sank lower in his chest.

When his call was transferred to voice mail, he didn't bother leaving a message.

The next time she looked at her phone, she would see that he'd called. The question was, would she care?

Poppy staggered into the house to find her mom folding laundry in the living room, and collapsed onto a chair.

"I was getting concerned. It gets dark so early these days, and I knew you were on the road and you were probably tired, what with not coming home all night . . ."

For once in her life, Poppy was in no mood for chitchat. The look on her face when she lolled her head toward Mom must've made that clear, because she let her worried rant taper off unfinished.

"When will they let you know?"

"They said they'd text us tomorrow or the next day."

"Saturday—your class reunion. Don't you think you should reconsider going? It's all anyone's been talking about for months. I hear they're expecting a high turnout. Even old Mr. Lu is driving over from where he retired in Hood River. He was always such a nice man. Not like that mean Ms. Baker."

She should have known her mom wouldn't be able to stop talking. Like mother, like daughter.

After last night, the very mention of partying made her head hurt even more. "Thanks for reminding me. The chance of running into her would be enough to keep me home even if I were thinking about going, which I'm not."

"Are you sure? Saturday might be the last time you see your old friends for a while. What about Heath? Is he going?"

With a supreme effort, she hoisted herself out of the easy chair. "Not a chance. He doesn't like crowds."

That was why he built that showplace right next door to his old house. It was like leaving home without really leaving.

"Is that so bad?"

"No guts, no glory," she muttered. She was so tired, she was talking gibberish.

"Now, I don't know if I'd call that fair. What with Heath's brewery being the talk of the town, I'd say he's got lots of glory."

"Heath has only ever done what comes naturally. He has a head for chemistry. So he made beer. Turned out he had a good business mind, too. Even though he was successful, he never had to stretch."

"That sounds pretty harsh."

"I know. I'm sorry. I'm babbling."

Mom put her hands on her hips. "Did something happen between you two? Because that would be awful, to leave Clarkston on bad terms with your best—"

"Mom. I'm sorry, but I'm beat. I'm going to go lie down."

"Do you want me to wake you up later so you can eat something?"

She felt her blood pressure rising. She didn't want to be coddled. She wanted rest and to be left alone. And later, time to think, to sort things out. "If I'm hungry, I'll get something myself."

But as she lay in her bedroom surrounded by relics of her childhood, sleep evaded her.

Where had that cutting comment about Heath's glory not being earned come from? What gave her the right to judge?

Then it came to her.

Whether or not she passed that test, she had left Portland that afternoon a different person. She had taken a chance, risked all or nothing. And it felt good. No matter what happened next, a new feeling filled her that she hadn't been able to give a name to, until now.

That feeling was *pride*.

Chapter Eighteen

Heath tried calling Poppy again later that evening, but he still couldn't reach her.

By the next morning, he couldn't wait any longer. He had to set some things straight.

He drove to her house and rapped on her door.

Right now, she should be getting ready for her lunch shift. Her parents would already be at the café, serving breakfast. This was the best time to catch her alone.

Their eyes met on opposite sides of the storm door window. But she made no move to let him in.

Jackson, the Springers' chocolate Lab, lifted his lip in an imitation of a snarl.

Inside the pockets of his jeans, Heath's hands clenched and unclenched. He'd never been a violent man. But dog or no dog, if he had to, he'd rip that door off its hinges.

He counted his exhalations as they condensed into fog: one, two, three . . .

That's it.

He rattled the handle. Locked.

Jackson barked a warning.

Alarm came over Poppy's face, then something like remorse—or was it pity? Whatever it was, she walked over and unlocked the door with a flick of her fingertip, leaving him to let himself in.

"Good dog," Heath said, giving Jackson a pat. The dog licked his hand and walked off.

"How'd it go?" he asked without preamble.

"It was good," she said tersely. "Your tutoring helped me a lot. I wanted to be sure to remember to tell you that."

He nodded, grateful for the crumbs she'd tossed him. "Glad I could help."

She wiped a sponge around the inside of a coffee cup, still obviously less than thrilled about him showing up unannounced.

"I tried calling you."

"I know."

He sighed and scrubbed a hand over his three-day beard.

"When do you find out?"

"Today or tomorrow. They'll text me."

He nodded again. *Really, I'm a stellar conversationalist.*

She held up a dripping plate while he stood there still in his jacket like the uninvited guest that he was.

Poppy pulled off her yellow rubber gloves and edged toward the hallway leading to the back of the house. "I have to get dressed for work, so . . ."

"I messed up."

She didn't respond.

She wasn't making this easy.

"We had a good time. I read more into it. I had this idiot notion that maybe now you . . ."

He hesitated. This was one of the hardest things he'd ever said.

He took her hands in his, drawing on her strength.

". . . you'd change your mind about leaving."

Whatever he'd said, it had broken through some icy barrier. Her expression softened. "Oh, Heath. You know why I have to leave. It has nothing to do with you. It's about me finding out who I am. What I'm capable of."

"Poppy," he beseeched her. "I'm obsessed. I can't work. I can't eat. You're all I think about. All I smell. You're in my tree house. You're in my living room." He lowered his voice. "In my bed."

She pulled her hands free, put them to her head, and shut her eyes. "Don't . . ."

She paced as far as the small room would allow, then whirled toward him, her hand on her heart. "If anyone knows how hard I've worked to pass this test, it's you. Do you really expect me to just give it all up because we made love one time?"

A muscle in Heath's face twitched as if he'd been slapped. After a moment, he lifted his chin. "You're right," he said. "I'd never want to make you change for me."

"Thank you. Thanks for understanding. But now I really have to get dressed, or I'm going to be late for work."

"Just one more thing."

Her shoulders sagged as she let out a held breath.

"Go to the reunion with me."

"Heath, I—"

"Please."

"You mean, like, together? As a couple?"

"As whatever you like. We don't have to define it. Nobody but us knows anything's changed between us."

To his profound relief, she seemed to weigh the idea. "You were probably supposed to let them know you were coming a month ago."

"Like Demi won't let us in. It's thanks to me she got her trees."

"Demi," she muttered. "I still don't know if I passed my test."

Her old insecurities were still with her. She was still scared Demi would call her out for being a loser.

"I knew it was a long shot." He kicked the floor with the toe of his boot. "I just thought, since there's a chance you might be heading out, you might want to see people for the last time . . ."

They stood there, the ticking of the Springers' old-fashioned wall clock filling the awkward silence.

Toast popped up, making them both jump. But Poppy didn't make a move.

Heath nodded toward the toaster. "Your toast's going to get cold. Then the butter won't melt, and you'll have those hard lumps—"

"It's not important."

"Yeah."

This was going nowhere.

The chivalrous thing to do was let her off the hook so she could stop struggling to think of the letdown line that sounded least like a kiss-off.

"I'll let you get ready for work then."

He turned and reached for the doorknob.

"Heath."

He looked over his shoulder. Her face, contorted with emotion, was heartbreakingly beautiful. How had it taken him so long to see the woman she had become? If he searched the world over, he would never find another like her.

His pulse pounded like thunder, waiting to hear what she would say.

"I'll go with you."

Confetti falling, angels singing.

"You will?"

She smiled weakly. "I don't know how I did yesterday. Maybe I passed, maybe I didn't. But two things I'll always have are, one, I gave that test everything in me. And two, I'll never stop being grateful to you for your help.

"So, if you're willing to brave a crowd for me, I guess I can handle a little razzing about being just a waitress."

Chapter Nineteen

On the night of the reunion, Demi Barnes was taking tickets at the door. "Poppy? I almost didn't recognize you without your little waitress uniform." Demi's stony glare expanded to include Heath. "You *do* know what RSVP means?" she added pointedly. "I can't guarantee you a meal."

The two of them peered past Demi into a room filled with people who all seemed to be talking at once.

A hand waved frantically. "Poppy!"

Poppy rose to her toes to try to see over the heads of the crowd. "It's Mona Cruz!" she exclaimed, excitedly waving back in the vicinity of where Mona's curly, dark head had last bobbed.

Heath hesitated. To him, that crowd meant hours of fumbled attempts at small talk.

"Not to late too change your mind," Poppy said into his neck, low enough that Demi couldn't hear.

He straightened up to his full height. "Nope," he said, handing Demi his credit card. "We're going all the way tonight. That is—"

Demi rolled her eyes. "Some things never change. Coatroom's on your right. Extra charge for the leather wine gourds on the table to your left."

Together, they moved forward. The restaurant had been transformed into a Roman garden. Gold and white fabric draped the walls, and flaming torches lit up the corners and tabletops.

With a hand on the small of her back, Heath guided Poppy around one of the potted saplings he had helped his dad deliver earlier that day.

Then they saw the surreal sight of their own images as they walked in projected onto a big screen at the far end of the room.

"Yas, Queen!" It was Keval, bowing to Poppy in pretend reverence, surrounded by a half dozen mutual friends. "Stop being so fabulous. Just stop." He scrutinized her little black dress. "I can't believe you came! Why didn't you tell me? You could have sat at our table."

"We can squeeze them in," said Junie.

"Yeah, no problem," said Sam with a hug for Poppy and a hearty pump of Heath's hand. "Glad you could make it, man."

"Look!" Rory pointed to the screen.

Heath was horrified to see a still photo of him in ninth grade wearing oversized lab goggles, pouring a solution into a construction paper cone that was taller than he was.

Here and there around the room, people pointed and laughed.

Heath prayed for a hole to open up and swallow him.

"What were you doing that day?" asked Rory.

"I was trying to see how high I could make a rocket fly using varying ratios of baking soda to vinegar."

"I remember that! It went up about twenty-five feet before it crashed. That was so cool."

"Could always count on you for one good explosion a week," said Sam. "Ol' Thompson thought it was her teaching that made chem so popular. It was because no one wanted to miss Heath's experiments."

Heath grinned. *Maybe this won't be so bad after all.*

A server in a toga waltzed by holding a platter aloft. "Hot oatcakes with honey?"

"When in Rome," quipped Red, helping herself. "Poppy, how'd you do on your test?"

Heath busied himself examining his oatcake.

"I'm waiting to find out any minute. They said I'd know by the end of today."

Red squeezed Poppy's arm. "That's so exciting!" Her hand slid down to Poppy's fingertips. "I see you still have all your nails. That's a good sign."

"Actually, I feel surprisingly calm."

"As you should. No matter what happens, you made a plan, took a risk. That's the place where personal growth comes from."

Junie looked up at the new video on the screen and nudged Heath. "Remember that night?"

Homecoming. Heath and Rory were cracking up at some long-forgotten joke. Heath wasn't going to go, but Poppy had nagged him until he finally caved.

"You always made sure I was included."

In the press of people, no one saw Poppy link her little finger with his. The tiny gesture made his chest swell.

"Want something from the bar?"

"Not just now. You go ahead."

"I think I'll have a beer," he said, extricating his finger with regret. "Be right back."

Heath disappeared, and a curly-haired brunette in a gaily patterned dress that set off her generous curves took his place.

"Poppy?"

"Mona!"

"You remembered me!"

How could she forget? Not many Clarkston High students had had a baby when they were still teenagers.

"Of course. How's your little boy?"

"Manuel's going into middle school next year, and Miguel's nine."

"That's impossible!"

Mona laughed. "I love being a mom. Keeps you young. I've been following your quest to become a wine steward on social media. What's the latest? Have you taken your test yet?"

"Just this week." She held up crossed fingers. "On pins and needles waiting to hear how I did."

"You must be going out of your mind! Talk about life-changing. Well, I'm rooting for you. I always knew you had it in you."

"I appreciate the vote of confidence. What are you up to these days? Last I heard you were living in California."

"I spent a few years trying to find myself. But you know what they say—there's no place like home. I realized I wanted to raise my boys here. So I came back. Got my business degree online," she boasted. "Took me six years, but now I'm home and looking for a job."

"What do you want to do?"

She shrugged. "Nice thing about a business degree is that it's flexible. I'd like to work around people. Thing is, not everyone is brave enough to take on a high school dropout."

"I'm sure you'll find something soon. You were always so—"

"Flirtatious?" Mona laughed.

"I was going to say personable."

Mona laughed again. "You're sweet."

"Well, anyway. I'm sure I'll be seeing—" But no. Poppy wouldn't be seeing Mona around—not if she got the news she was hoping for. She wouldn't be seeing much of anyone in this room, in this town, anymore.

Daryl Decaprio was tugging Mona toward the dance floor.

"You've still got it going on," Poppy said in Mona's ear.

"And *you*," Mona pointed at Poppy, "were always more than just the prom queen." She winked and was gone, Sam and Red following close on her heels.

Standing next to Poppy was Junie, watching the couples having fun with a wistful expression. A year ago, Sam had hired Manolo Santos to oversee the building of the new wine consortium. But once Manolo met Junie, he ended up spending as much time whipping her place into shape as he did on Sam's project. When the fall crush started, her new tasting room and patio brought the tourists in droves. And then, like a brownie who helps with household tasks overnight and then vanishes at dawn, Manolo was gone.

Poppy knew Junie still missed the engineer who wasn't ready to settle down.

Without saying a word, Keval offered Junie his elbow and escorted her onto the dance floor.

Mona was right, thought Poppy. Clarkston was special. It would always hold a place in her heart.

Heath rejoined Poppy at the same time as Sandy Houser. "Poppy! Kyle and I were so sad when we heard you're leaving town. The café won't be the same without you."

Poppy brightened at the compliment.

She wants this so much, Heath thought. What was more, she deserved it. How could he stand in her way?

"How soon are you leaving?"

"I'm still waiting for all the pieces to fall into place, but assuming they do, right away."

"You have to promise me you'll come back for my baby shower in February."

She flushed with pleasure. "I'll move heaven and earth to be there."

Watching the Housers melt into the crowd, Poppy gushed, "I didn't know Sandy cared. I thought was just the person who poured her coffee and brought her eggs."

"A lot of people care." He tipped her chin. "You really have no clue, do you?"

"I always tried to be extra nice to people, to make up for not seeming to be too smart. But that doesn't mean it wasn't real. I couldn't fake it if I didn't feel it inside."

He gave her a side hug. "Glad you came?"

"You know what? I really am."

"Me too."

The fast song ended and a slow one began.

Her eyes sparkled up at him. "Remember this one?"

The theme song to their prom. How could he forget? And though they'd gone to that event as a group, not a couple, at the end of the night, Poppy had pulled him out onto the dance floor.

Heath put his hand lightly on her waist, and she took his cue and turned into him. He closed his eyes, blocking out the sight of the jam-packed room, and savored the feel of Poppy's body as he let the lyrics flow through him.

First time we danced I knew I needed you so . . .

After the other morning, he was afraid he might never hold Poppy again. But she was right: Yesterday was gone, and the future was unknown. All they had was now, and he was determined to make the most of it.

At first, he was careful to keep his hands within the safe bounds of her back, waist, and shoulders. He didn't want to blow it for the second time in three days.

But when he felt her relax against him he got braver, cradling the sides of her rib cage, letting the tips of his thumbs graze the under-swell of her breasts. He waited for her to freeze up. But when she closed her eyes and laid her head on his shoulder, it made him feel like a man, powerful and protective and wanted.

And even then I knew I'd never let you go.

She lifted her head and he drew back to read her face.

At her lazy, seductive smile, her liquid blue eyes, he thought his heart might burst.

The crowd faded away. He cupped the back of her head, stroking the long, silken strands, and breathed in the scent of her.

You're so intoxicating . . . I know I won't stop waiting . . .

Without her, he could never be whole.

I'll be anticipating . . . 'cause I love you so.

As the final line was being sung, Heath probed Poppy's eyes, hoping beyond hope that the song's sentiment meant something to her, too. But at the same moment, he felt a tap on his shoulder.

"I just wanted you to know, I made sure they made a meal for you two."

It was the caterer.

"Is this your date?"

"Er, yes. This is Poppy."

"Poppy? Liz. I met Heath when he and his dad dropped off the trees. Turns out Scott and I went to school together."

"It was nice of you to fit us in at the last minute."

"Glad I found you. They just started plating the chicken Vesuvio."

With fingers intertwined as tightly as their lives, he and Poppy wove through the crush of bodies to their table full of friends.

Before dessert was served, Red whispered something in Poppy's ear.

"Be right back," Poppy told Heath, setting her phone next to her plate.

Heath followed Poppy with his eyes as she and Red walked away, gabbing.

"What's with women that they can't pee alone?" asked Sam irreverently.

Heath grinned. "Can't stop talking that long."

"That reminds me. You ever give Poppy back her wine?"

Heath swigged his beer and nodded.

"And? Come on, man. Throw me a bone. I saw you two out there," he said, indicating the dance floor with his chin.

"Why do you care? What's my love life to you?"

"I thought we had a pact? I give you some pointers, then, once we get you squared away, we start working on me."

"Something tells me you don't need my help."

"Ha! My reputation precedes me."

As if to prove his point, an attractive woman materialized on the other side of Sam, diverting his attention.

At the same time, Keval appeared at Heath's shoulder. "I have to go take care of business. There're a couple of people who couldn't make it, but they wanted to share a video message. If I'm not back when the server brings the baklava, will you make sure he doesn't bypass me?"

On the table, Poppy's phone blinked. *Congratulations. This is to notify you that you have earned certified sommelier status. For more details on your score, please click on the link.*

Heath's eyes froze on the screen. He'd been suppressing thoughts of that test all night. But there was no escaping it now.

Keval had seen the text too. His eyes grew round as quarters. "Poppy is going to shit rainbows."

Damn Keval's sweet tooth. If not for that, he and Poppy might have had one more spin around the dance floor. One more blissful hour, before he lost her forever.

Heath's heart pounded . . . his thoughts raced. A secret wasn't a secret if more than one person knew it. And if one of those people happened to be a social media maven—

"Well? Are you going to tell her, or should I?" Keval prompted.

There was no denying it now. This was it. Poppy was on her way out of town, out of his life. And just like Sam said, Heath had practically shown her the door.

He'd been working on making this a reality, but that didn't stop his world from falling apart now that it had.

"Go," he told Keval. "Take care of your business. I'll show her as soon as she gets back, and then you two can figure out how to handle it from there."

This was too big to keep quiet for long. Within minutes of Poppy finding out, the story would be on the lips of every person at the reunion.

But it wouldn't stop at the border of Clarkston. Cory Anthony and Palette had a stake in Poppy's results, too. Whatever else they were doing tonight, whatever ritzy venue they were dining at or far-flung party they were attending, Heath bet they were keeping one eye on their devices. It wouldn't take much for Keval to get them to give Poppy her due, in public, on the reunion's big screen.

Soon, everyone in the room would be clamoring to get next to her . . . showering her with hugs and good wishes. For once in her life, she would be the belle of the ball—for her brains, not her beauty.

Maybe she would finally find the happiness that eluded her.

Resigned, Heath rose to look in the direction she'd gone off in just in time to spy her on her way back to him, glowing . . . exuberant . . . surrounded by longtime friends. He took a mental snapshot, preserving that sight forever in his mind. It was the last time she would be known as Poppy Springer, café waitress. After tonight, she would be Poppy Springer, Certified Sommelier and Face of Palette Cosmetics.

As she glided toward the table, he opened his arms to her.

She smiled quizzically. "What's this about?" she asked as her body met his.

"Congratulations, baby," he breathed into her hair. "You did it."

It seemed as though the congratulations would go on forever. Twice, Demi had announced that the party was over, to no avail.

Heath was standing against the wall watching Poppy accept yet more accolades when he spotted Demi badgering the headwaiter.

When she caught Heath's eye, she left the poor man standing there helplessly and marched over to him.

"Look," Demi said, pointing to her watch. "This event was officially over fifteen minutes ago, per our agreement with the restaurant. The waitstaff needs to clean this mess up and get it ready for tomorrow's business. You need to help me get these people out of here. They won't listen to me."

"I'm not part of your committee."

"But that's your—*friend* over there who's holding things up."

Heath followed Demi's angry glare to the circle of admirers surrounding Poppy. Soon enough, she would be separated from them. It would be hard for her, even if it was her own doing.

"I'll see what I can do."

A possible solution came to mind, but it was way out of his wheelhouse. He hesitated.

A couple of servers started going from table to table, putting out the torches. Time was running out.

That firmed Heath's resolve. He worked his way around the edge of the crowd, spreading the word.

When he told Sam what the plan was, Sam whisked a torch out of a server's hand and held it high. "After-party at Heath Sinclair's!" he shouted.

The cry went up around the room. "Party at Heath's!"

Poppy found Heath as she was coming back from the coat check. "Is it true? You're offering up your house for an after-party?"

He held her coat for her to slip into. "We'd better get going if we're going to beat the horde."

"Hold on! My bag's at the table."

She scurried back for it while Heath waited, thinking ahead. He had a lot to do to get ready.

Someone stopped the music, midsong. By now the only people remaining were Demi and the waitstaff. Even Jess, Demi's sidekick, had abandoned her for Heath's house.

Poppy caught up with Heath, only to pause again at the exit.

"Forget something else?"

Pressing her lips together, she turned and went back to where Demi was balling up a soiled tablecloth.

"Do you want to come with us to the after-party, Demi?" he heard her ask.

Demi's expression ran the gamut of emotions, from bitter, to tempted, and finally, back to her true north.

"No, thank you," she spat.

"Okay, then. The reunion was wonderful. You did a great job," said Poppy.

She turned and, giving Heath her arm and her winning smile, said, "Now, let's go."

Chapter Twenty

Poppy peered over Junie's shoulder where Heath was mixing drinks at his kitchen island. A dozen bottles littered the counters, surrounded with lemon and lime halves and empty cracker boxes on their sides.

"Did you hear what I said?" asked Junie over the speakers blasting one of Heath's playlists.

Poppy turned her attention back to the noisy living room. There were people everywhere, christening Heath's furniture, congregating on both sides of the fireplace.

"You asked when I was leaving. We're scheduled to start training on Monday. There'll be a soft opening a week later, followed by the real thing in early January."

"What about Christmas? It's less than three weeks away."

"I'll come home. We always have the Sinclairs over. Can't miss that."

"Good. Heath's really going to miss you, you know."

She swallowed a hard lump in her throat. "I'm going to go check and see if he needs any help."

Keval's widespread arms blocked her path. In one hand a tall glass dangled perilously.

"Mwah. Mwah." He air kissed Poppy's cheeks, then draped an arm around her shoulders. "Everyone is so proud of you, Poppykins. How exciting was that when Cory Anthony himself congratulated you right there on the screen at the reunion, in front of all those people?"

"It was amazing. Thank you so much for making that happen."

He took a swig of his drink. "I owed you for live-streaming that disastrous first tasting. I never should have done that. Can you forgive me?"

"There's nothing to forgive." She smiled and ducked under his arm. "I was just on my way to see Heath."

"Get him to make you one of these," he called after her, lifting his drink.

She found Heath holding a blender in his hands—while it was running.

Poppy picked up an egg from the open carton lying next to the blender. "What is that?" she yelled over the roar.

"Gin fizz," said Kyle Houser happily.

"With eggs?"

Heath lowered the blender, pressed stop, and peeled off the lid.

"Egg whites, simple syrup, lemon, lime, and soda water."

"Do you have to hold it while it's running? Seems a little—risky."

"Lifting it up while it's blending stretches and folds the protein molecules of the albumin in the egg white, trapping air. That's what gives it its foamy consistency."

He poured the frothy mixture into a glass for Kyle, reserving a little for her.

"Here. Try some."

"That's okay. I'll stick with wine."

Kyle drifted back to the living room, leaving the two of them alone in the kitchen until the next thirsty guest came back for a refill.

"How are you doing?" Poppy asked as Heath rinsed out the blender under the tap.

"Turns out parties aren't half-bad when I have something to do. Especially when I get to throw in a little chemistry."

Of course. The role of bartender was made for Heath.

"I know this isn't easy. Getting the news at the reunion . . . inviting all these people over to your place so you could keep the party going, just for me. That was really big of you."

"You've always been there for me."

His crooked smile touched her soul.

She stole a quick kiss. "We'll talk before I leave. Okay?"

He busied himself setting the blender back on its base.

She cocked her head, searching his face as he wiped his hands on a dish towel.

"Okay?" she repeated.

Heath put his hands around her waist, pulled her close, and brought his mouth squarely down on hers.

Celebrating her achievement . . . opening up his very private world to the masses . . . and now kissing her, not caring who might walk in? Maybe she wasn't the only one who was changing.

Much later, Heath locked the door behind the last departing guest and rambled over to where Poppy was stacking the dishwasher.

"That can wait," he said, removing a glass from her hand, leading her out of the kitchen. "Come to bed."

The next morning, Heath felt the mattress sink.

"Heath."

He opened one eye.

Perched next to him with one leg tucked beneath her was a gorgeous, blue-eyed blonde.

He smiled and reached out to pull her back down into the sheets.

"I can't." She edged away. "I have a million and one things to do. Call the Realtor, talk to Cory and Palette, pack, sit down with my mom and Big Pop . . . they don't even know yet, and they're probably wringing their hands wondering what's going on . . ."

Know what? He blinked her into focus. In the harsh light of morning, last night's party dress looked gaudy and out of place.

He stretched to his full length and yawned. "What time is it?"

"Almost eleven," she said hurriedly. "I let your dogs out and fed Vienna and did a quick once-over of the downstairs, but . . ."

He propped himself up on his elbows, trying to piece together the details of last night. Happy as he was to be waking up to Poppy, something lurked around the edges of his consciousness. Something ominous.

"I'm going to have to leave the rest of the mess to you."

"No. It's okay. Do what you have to do."

She frowned. "Can you run me home? All I have are these." She dangled a pair of high heels by their straps.

"Oh. Right."

She rose and stood by his bed, waiting with barely disguised impatience.

"Thanks for understanding," she said as he put his feet on the floor.

By the time he pulled on a pair of jeans and a shirt, she was already waiting by the door with her coat on.

"Got time for a cup of coffee?" he asked, trying to put off the inevitable. Still pretending that the world as they knew it wasn't about to come crashing to an end.

"I already had some."

In the car, she said, "I owe you. I'll get some cash from the machine and run it over later."

He frowned. "For what?"

"Last night. You went through a lot of booze."

"Poppy, I don't want your money."

"You sure? I want to chip in."

He shook his head at the very idea.

He was wide awake by the time he pulled into her driveway under gray skies.

"See ya," she said, jumping out almost before his car had stopped.

As she scampered around the hood, he slid down his window. "Call me," he reminded her as she slipped into her house.

She waved distractedly, as if he were already a distant memory.

When she shut the door to her house, he felt like he'd been shut out of her life.

After last night's festivities, his house seemed even quieter than usual. It took until afternoon to clean up the mess. Then he ran a load of laundry, washed his car, bought a precooked chicken to share with his dad.

But behind the veneer of his Sunday routine, the hours dragged by in a surreal haze. He pictured Poppy breaking the news to her parents and he tried to imagine what they were going through, wanting the best for their only child, even if it meant losing her.

He had never felt closer to them in spirit.

At least once every hour he checked his phone to make sure he hadn't missed Poppy's call.

When Dad retreated to his den, he drove to the deserted brewery and wandered around like a ghost, checking on things that didn't need checked. Finally he sat down at his desk where, before the reunion, he'd been in the midst of planning the year ahead.

He thought of how lucky he was. The business was going great guns. He and his team had exciting stuff in the pipeline: a great new Bavarian-style wheat beer, a beautifully polished pale ale. He should be on top of the world.

His seat creaked in the silence when he got up, shoved his hands in his pockets, and peered out the window. The sun had refused to show his face all day, as if he, too, were brooding.

Last night had been lit up with artificial lights, music, and good cheer. But now the winter solstice, the darkest time of the year, approached.

Chapter Twenty-one

Hours after she broke the news, Poppy's parents still looked shell-shocked.

Neither of them had to work today, so they wandered around like lost sheep, bumping into each other, trying to help Poppy but only managing to get in her way.

Tossing clothes into piles, she heard the house phone ring.

"Poppy?" Mom called from the living room. "It's a reporter from the *NewsRegister*. Can you come to the phone?"

A reporter? She dropped what she was doing to talk to him. Wait until Demi Barnes and mean old Mrs. Baker and any other naysayers read this!

A while later, the doorbell rang.

"Who can that be on a Sunday afternoon?" Mom fretted.

It was a deliveryman with a long box full of orange flowers.

"Who are they from?" Mom hovered over her as she opened the card.

There was no message, just a name.

Poppy looked up, eyes misting. "Heath."

Mom's hand flew to her breast. "Poppies, this time of year? They must have come all the way from Holland. Can you imagine? Do you want me to put them in a vase for you?"

Afraid to speak for fear her voice would crack, she handed them over gratefully. Dwelling on Heath while she was trying to get ready to leave town was counterproductive, she thought, with a twinge of guilt. Going back down the hall to her room turned upside down, she pushed his touching gesture out of her mind.

Then an assistant from the cosmetics company called, transforming Poppy's guilt into self-satisfaction.

"Congratulations! We've been following your progress, and we're so happy to welcome you as the official face of Palette!"

All her efforts were paying off—and then some.

"We think your look personifies the Palette woman. Now for the details. Dieter will be your trainer. He'll be waiting for you tomorrow at six a.m. sharp."

"Pardon?" Her own personal trainer? She stood sideways in the full-length mirror at her slightly pouty tummy and tried, unsuccessfully, to suck it all in.

"I thought I was supposed to be the Face of Palette Cosmetics. Not the body."

"We don't want chipmunk cheeks, do we? Dieter's the top trainer in Portland, and he has cleared his calendar for us. Per your contract, you will be meeting with him on a regular basis."

"But I'll have to leave Clarkston at four thirty to get there by six."

"As I said, it's in the contract we faxed you. You did read it?"

All that fine print? It would have taken her days.

She swallowed her misgivings. Mandatory workouts were a small price to pay for having everything you ever wanted, she supposed.

Next, her new boss called to tell her there was a staff meeting at one o'clock tomorrow, followed by a tour of the new facility and a celebratory dinner at a place so exclusive, Poppy had never dreamed she would ever get to go there. Now she was going as a guest of her VIP boss, at his expense.

If this was any indication of what her new life was going to be like, those workouts might come in handy.

"There's this great Bordeaux-style blend from the coast of Tuscany that I want your opinion on," said Cory. "It's among the top ten Italian—"

Her phone vibrated. *Heath.* She was supposed to have called him.

Her eye landed on Heath's stuffed dog in a box atop a stack of folded sheets.

The phone buzzed again, and her blood pressure ratcheted up.

Cory—he'd insisted she start calling him by his first name—was still talking about the wine list. She couldn't interrupt him by accepting another call. In fact, she should be paying careful attention what he was saying. She would be expected to remember it tomorrow.

No sooner had the buzzing finally stopped and Cory's words

started making sense again than her father appeared in the doorway, tapping his foot.

"I can't get the right size U-Haul until Thursday," he said when she hung up. "Why don't you just commute until then? If you don't, you're going to have to sleep on your floor until I can get your bed delivered."

It had been a long day in the Springer household. Nerves were frayed.

"You don't have to do that, Big Pop. I told you, I'll buy a new bed."

"Oh, I see, Miss Big Spender. Are you planning on buying a whole houseful of new furniture, all at once? You at least need your chest of drawers..."

Her head was spinning.

"Pop! Let me figure it out, okay?"

He threw up his hands and disappeared, muttering to himself.

It wasn't the right time to call Heath back.

Nor was it time later, either, when she finally caved to her mom's nagging to sit down and eat her favorite vegetable soup, made from scratch.

After that, she still had to decide what clothes she couldn't live without until her next trip back to Clarkston. She'd never been that into clothes, yet suddenly, nothing she owned seemed good enough.

When she was startled awake by yet another call, the sky outside her bedroom window was pitch black.

She hoisted herself onto an elbow, wincing at muscles unaccustomed to bedroom aerobics and dancing and dozens of trips out to her tiny Mini Cooper to stuff it with as many of her belongings as would fit.

In the glow of her pink ceramic lamp with butterflies cavorting on it, her stripped-down room looked eerily unfamiliar. That lamp was definitely *staying*.

"You awake?"

"Heath." Her hand flew to her forehead. "I'm sorry."

There was silence on the other end. She'd meant to call him hours ago. By now he might be pacing in the dark in front of one of his floor-to-ceiling windows, or seated spread-legged on the edge of his black leather couch in one of his collection of faded T-shirts, patiently waiting for her call before going to bed.

"You said we could talk."

"I know," she sighed heavily. "It's just that today was so intense. Trying to pack with reporters calling, Cory calling, my parents driving me nuts..."

"Scarlett and Big Pop just want what's best for you."

"I know."

"You all set?"

"I think so. I don't know. I fell asleep on the floor."

"Been an eventful twenty-four hours."

Her defenses, always close to the surface lately, bobbed up again. "You say that like it's a bad thing."

Immediately, she regretted her words. "I didn't mean to sound snippy."

Heath didn't deserve that, especially after all he'd done for her. But her whole life was about to change, and she had decisions to make and people were pulling her in different directions.

"This is the best thing that's happened to me in a long time."

It was his turn to say he knew.

"The best thing *ever*, come to think of it."

Stung, Heath considered where he would rank making love with Poppy in the bigger scheme of things. Above his career success, for sure.

"I never want to go back to being a loser again," she was saying.

"'Loser?' What about your party, after the reunion? No one there ever thought you were a loser. The only one who ever said that was Demi, and not even she believed it. She was just jealous because of some imagined shortcoming of her own."

"Well, I grew up thinking they did."

He rubbed a spot on the leather couch where someone had spilled something the night before. "I guess perception is reality."

"Look, Heath," she said with a sudden urgency in her voice. "Why don't you come with me?"

He knew her so well. Well enough to know that this was only last-minute jitters talking.

"This is my home. I belong here."

"Remember what that brewmaster said the day we went up to Portland? They would welcome you like a hero. You'd fit right in."

"Clarkston suits me fine."

"It'd be so much fun! Think of all the things we could do to-gether," she prattled on, ignoring his protests. "A different restaurant every night. The clubs, the shops, the museums . . ."

"Aren't you going to be working most nights and weekends?"

That gave her pause. "I won't be working twenty-four seven."

"What about the modeling gig? When are you going to fit that in?"

"Cory will give me time off for that. He says the extra publicity for the restaurant will be worth it."

" 'Cory,' is it? What happened to 'Chef'?"

"All his employees call him by his first name."

Her irrational idea combined with his fatigue was starting to wear on him. This conversation was all wasted breath. Poppy was facing a big, scary change, and she wanted her hand held. But their days of al-ternating favors were over. Now they had each finally arrived—at separate destinations.

"You can't have it both ways, Poppy. I'm not moving to Portland when everything I love is here."

Still, he refused to let things end on a low note.

"We'll stay in touch," he said, though deep down he feared the opposite, that they would drift apart. It was probably inevitable.

"Of course we will. I'll call you—"

Like you promised to call me today? The same thought was in each of their minds, and they both knew it.

"Think of me," he blurted, casting aside the last remnant of his pride.

"I have to do this," she choked.

This was really the end, this time.

There in his dark, cavernous house, Heath scrubbed a hand through his hair. He had no choice but to let her go. She needed him to believe in her, not add to her self-doubt.

"I'll come see you once in a while."

"Sure you will," she sniffed. "We'll only be an hour away . . ."

With all of the commitments your new life entails? Might as well be a million miles.

". . . and I'll come back and see you, too. A lot. Or at least, as often as I can."

Heath fisted the phone so hard it was a wonder it didn't break in two, the way his heart was breaking. "And spend the night?"

"If you think I should," she replied, a soft smile in her voice.

Chapter Twenty-two

"Hup twenty-eight! Hup twenty-nine! Hup thirty! Ten-second break. You earned it."

Poppy dropped the medicine ball, careful not to let it crush her toes, bent over, and fought for breath. She wiped her brow and peered up through the sweat dripping in her eyes at the clock on the wall of the elite workout studio.

Fifteen minutes? That's all the time she'd been working out?

Then again, maybe if she broke a toe, she could get out of her contract.

"Break over! Did you hear me? I said, break over! *Pick up that ball.* Ready? Set? Hup one! Hup two . . ."

This must be what boot camp is like. She wished she'd had Heath read her that contract before she signed it.

"This is only our first day! I'm taking it easy on you!"

"How long"—*pant*—"do we have to do this?" Poppy managed to get out between reps.

Dieter circled her, noting her form with a critical eye. "Your company is very generous. They are paying me for three days a week for the length of your contract."

Holy hell. When she'd set out to become a sommelier, she'd had no idea she would end up lifting weights and doing lunges until her butt cheeks screamed.

Despite the workouts, those first few, glorious days in Portland, Poppy felt like a caged bird set free.

Which wasn't to say she didn't work as hard as she ever had. Cory Anthony ate, breathed, and slept the restaurant business, and he expected his employees to do the same. Though everyone on his staff had experience, he insisted on spending the next few weeks retraining them to meet his standards for the way a fine restaurant should be run.

Poppy and the other two other wine stewards—stern Morgan, with his dark suits, bow ties, and impressive background in some of the top restaurants in Chicago, and nervous Stuart, who sported an artsy glasses collection and was always showing off the latest photos of his new baby—soon came to the realization that Cory was obsessive about his wine list. There were endless tastings and lengthy meetings with distributors. Not only did Cory value their opinions, he made it clear that he expected them to be proactive in helping the list evolve.

That only made Poppy more proud of her new position.

On her only two free mornings of her first week in in her new apartment, she combed the home goods stores picking out throw rugs, houseplants, her first towels chosen without help from anyone. Little things that might not be a big deal to some, but to her were tangible proof of her growing independence.

Friday morning, she got home from her workout to find the U-Haul Big Pop had rented sitting in front of her apartment.

Surprised at how much she'd missed her father, she ran over to where he slid open the back door of the vehicle and threw her arms around him.

"How's it going, my girl?" he asked, the tension of their last day together long forgotten.

"I missed you!" she blurted.

"You did?" he replied with undisguised pleasure that produced a lump in Poppy's throat. "I missed you, too." He cupped her chin in his work-worn hand and squinted down at her, his smile fading to concern. "What's that dirt under your eyes?"

"Nothing. Just a little smudge of mascara." She made a show of swiping a finger beneath a lower lid.

"Looks like someone's been burning the midnight oil."

"Maybe a little."

Big Pop averted his eyes. Mom was the established worrier queen. *His* role was smoothing over the inevitable mother-daughter tensions that arose from time to time.

"Got your mattress here. How'd you like sleeping on the floor the past few nights? Not much, by the looks of you."

"It wasn't bad at all," she lied. Between the harsh workouts and the long hours getting the restaurant ready for the grand opening, her body felt like one giant bruise.

"Might as well take this back, then," he said, pretending to yank down on the van's door.

"No!" she protested, laughing. "Let me help you carry my stuff in before I have to get ready for work."

Even a *little* furniture made her small place look as if it had shrunk.

After Big Pop positioned her bed, he stood back and looked around the space. "Too bad your mother couldn't come. She could have helped you figure out where to put all your knickknacks and so on better than I could. But someone had to work the lunch shift till we find a new hire."

The idea of someone else working so closely with her mom, day in and day out, almost made her jealous. *Ridiculous.*

"That's okay. I like deciding for myself where I want to put things."

"A little independence and you're craving more. Well, don't worry. I had a talk with her. Told her you're a grown woman now, wanting to stand on your own two feet. And it won't help for us to be showing up on your doorstep all the time uninvited."

"Aw, Big Pop. You know you're welcome any time. But do me a favor? If I look a little tired, don't mention it to Mom. I'll catch up on my rest now that you brought me this."

"You think I'm crazy? The woman worries enough for ten people as it is."

Over the weekend Poppy experimented with exactly where she wanted her eclectic combination of new and old, moving things around according to her whim: a sophisticated new lamp on her old chest of drawers . . . a framed photo of her parents in the living room.

Sunday night she crawled into her bed, looked around, and sighed with satisfaction.

But when she turned off her new lamp and curled Heath's dog into her chest, his parting words popped into her head.

Think of me.

She flipped onto her belly and tried to concentrate on the new chardonnay she wanted to put up for a vote to add to the wine list.

But she wasn't used to the sound of traffic right outside her window. So she switched to her other side, bunching her pillow over her exposed ear.

Think of me.

She had a full day tomorrow. If she'd learned one thing in her first week of working for Cory Anthony, it was that she had to be at her best at all times. She needed her rest.

Think of me.

The night before her test, when she and Heath had discovered a new, adult side of each other, came back to her. The feel of smooth skin stretched over taut muscle. The taste of his mouth. His easy grace . . . his unexpectedly sure hands.

She remembered how he looked the morning after, standing bare-chested in his driveway despite the cold, right after she'd turned down his offer of a partnership.

She turned onto her back again, coming full circle, inadvertently knocking Heath's dog to the floor in the process.

She sighed. *It can stay there.* Inhaling Heath's scent with every breath probably wasn't helping her any.

But she didn't have it in her to abandon a part of Heath, no matter how inanimate, on the floor all night. With a sigh of exasperation, she climbed out from under the covers to retrieve the dog, setting him far enough away so that she couldn't smell him, yet secure in the fact that he was there with her, and he was safe.

For the rest of the night, dreams of Heath wove in and out of fitful bouts of sleep.

Poppy started out with the best of intentions. She resolved to start checking her email and her friends' posts regularly, to keep up with the goings-on back in Clarkston, but she should have known she wouldn't have time for all that reading and writing. Talking had always been her preferred form of communication.

During those first few days, the thought of calling Heath was never far from Poppy's mind. But by the time she finally got home around one a.m., she knew he would be sleeping.

By Friday night, she couldn't wait any longer.

His voice was the sound of home. She fell back on her new couch and hugged a throw pillow, excited to share all the details of her new life.

"Cory is so smart and well-connected. He has all these dedicated customers from his other restaurants, and he's given them gift certificates to our new place, hoping that they'll eat here and talk it up."

"That *is* smart."

"He can be demanding. But then, I guess you have to have high expectations when you're running a business."

"I guess so."

She told him about Morgan's stiff formality and Stu's new baby, and how Cory was teaching the three of them to work as a cohesive team.

"Sounds like everything's going great," Heath said when she'd finally run out of steam.

"What about you? What's going on there?"

"Same old, same old. Ran into your mom at the café. She got her turkey for next week."

"Christmas is next week?" Poppy hadn't bought any presents. She hadn't baked chocolate chip cookies with Mom or helped Big Pop pick out the tree.

"Do you know when you're coming home yet?"

"I'm sure Cory will tell us soon. The soft opening is getting rave reviews. We're packed every night."

"You'll be home for Christmas Eve." It was a statement, not a question.

Ever since that awful year when Heath's mom left, the Springers had been inviting Heath and his dad to their place on Christmas Eve. Big Pop got fresh Tillamook Bay salmon from one of his suppliers. Mom cooked it using her special recipe. They washed it all down with Riesling from Washington State.

"Of course I'll be home! You can count on me."

After two weeks, Poppy knew where the best coffee shops were between her apartment and work and had memorized her way to the market and the stores that carried essentials like batteries, lightbulbs, and toiletries.

Now it was only two days until Christmas Eve. She couldn't wait to gather around the table with her parents and Heath, and even Heath's dad, quiet as he was. She had lots of stories to tell.

Cory was on yet another of his never-ending string of phone calls. While the staff waited for him to hang up and give them his last-minute instructions on the evening's dinner service, they chatted excitedly about their holiday plans. Stu, in particular, was beside himself. Instead of buying gifts, his parents, brothers, and sister had saved up to fly out from the East Coast to meet his new son. It would be the first time he'd seen his family in a year.

And Poppy thought *two weeks* away from home was a long time.

The table came to attention as Cory jammed his phone in his pocket and strode over to them wearing a serious expression.

"That was one of our backers. He wants us to cater a last-minute party at his house Christmas Eve."

Nobody breathed.

"I'm going to need three servers and two wine stewards."

He looked around the table expectantly.

"I'll tend bar," said Morgan. "Hanukkah's over."

Reluctantly, three servers' hands went up.

"That leaves either Poppy or Stu. Who's it going to be?" demanded Cory, eyes boring into theirs.

She couldn't wait to go home. She missed everything about Christmas in Clarkston: hauling the tree home with Big Pop, Mom's home cooking, exchanging wrapped gifts.

And she was dying to see Heath.

Stu's eyes pleaded with her.

She tried to imagine not seeing her loved ones for a whole year.

Of its own accord, her hand slowly climbed toward the ceiling.

Cory nodded curtly. "Those of you who volunteered, stay here to be filled in on the details. The rest of you can go set up for tonight's service."

Poppy placated her parents by promising to get up at the crack of dawn Christmas morning and spend the next two days with them.

Heath wasn't as easily appeased.

"I don't have to be back at work until the twenty-seventh. We can hang out Christmas afternoon. The day after, too, if you want."

"No, we can't. I've got Seahawks tickets."

"Football? On Christmas?"

"I've been trying to talk Dad into going to a game for a couple of years now. Finally got him to say yes."

That was not at all what she'd been expecting.

"But you'll be back the next day."

"First time Dad's been out of town in ages. I'd like to make the most of it, so we're going up early, on Christmas Day, and staying three nights in a hotel. We'll check out the Space Needle, the craft beer scene and Pike Place before the game. Then there's the three-hour drive back."

"By the time you get home, I'll be gone again."

"I'm sorry. You told me we were getting together Christmas Eve."

She had taken for granted that Heath would be available at her convenience.

"You there?"

"Yeah." Though shaken, she forced herself to sound cheerful. "That's nice that your dad wants to get out and do something fun with you."

"Remember Liz?"

"The caterer who made sure we didn't go hungry at our class reunion?"

"She must've lit a spark. Ever since the day he ran into her, something's different about him."

"I've only been gone a couple weeks, and already I'm out of the loop."

"A lot can happen in a couple weeks."

She wondered what else she'd missed.

"Well, at least I can wish you a Merry Christmas over the phone," she said wistfully.

"You can try. I'll probably be sticking pretty close to Dad. It's not often I can get him out of the house."

She detected an unmistakable chill in his tone.

"Heath, don't be mad."

"I *am* mad. You said you'd be here."

"It was either me or my coworker with a new baby and his family he hasn't seen in a year."

Heath sighed. "I guess you had no choice."

"I didn't. You would have done the same thing in my shoes."

"You're right. I would have."

But she hung up feeling even worse now that Heath had cut her some slack.

Well, she thought, she'd gotten exactly what she wanted. And now she had to live with it.

Chapter Twenty-three

Anthony's was a sensation.

Poppy's service skills were becoming honed to a fine edge. Now that she had a specialized skill, she found that patrons relied on her knowledge and point of view. People started asking for her by name. They wanted to be seen with her even outside the restaurant, so she got invited to more events and parties than she could possibly go to, even if Cory gave her time off for the ones that were corporately sponsored—those that showed the restaurant in a favorable light and garnered publicity.

If not for the regular workouts, she would almost have forgotten about the modeling gig, until the second week of January when Palette called to tell her they had scheduled her first photo shoot.

"How's Dieter treating you?" the woman asked familiarly, as if they were long-lost friends.

Poppy assured them she'd been working out regularly.

"I already know that. He checks in with us weekly to report on your progress."

Poppy was dumbstruck. She felt like a child being checked on, or worse, an animal being groomed for market. Before she could come up with a reply, the woman continued.

"You deserve a treat. How would you like to get a facial?"

"I've never had one."

"Let me give you the name of the aesthetician we use. Get in touch with her. Your first photo shoot is coming up a week from Wednesday."

That afternoon Poppy followed Cory into his office to tell him she needed next Wednesday off.

"You can't do that. A food blogger is coming for a private tour of the kitchen before we open. Tell them you'll have to reschedule."

"But I thought you said—"

"Not happening," he said with finality. "You're a professional sommelier first. If not for that fact, Palette Cosmetics would have no use for you. They'll have to schedule your modeling assignments when you're not needed here."

He pulled out his phone to bark at his supplier about a shipment of dishware was that was supposed to have been delivered last week.

The aesthetician was an ice-blonde named Olga.

"Sit."

Poppy did as she was told.

Abruptly, Olga inclined Poppy's chair backward until her blood rushed to her head, feeling for all the world like she was being prepped for a root canal.

There was a burst of white light. When Poppy's pupils had contracted sufficiently, she pried her lids open to see a distorted eyeball peering down at her through a big round lens mounted on a swinging arm. Something pinched her cheek and she winced, and the eye in the lens frowned in disapproval.

"Have you heard of sunscreen?"

"Of course." She'd never made a habit of actually *using* it, but that wasn't the question.

Olga slapped a bottle into her hand. "You need to start Palette's retinol product to slough off those dead cells. You're getting a late start, but better late than never."

"I'm only twenty-eight."

"You have the pores of a woman ten years older."

Poppy didn't want to risk Cory's displeasure by asking again for time off to do her first photo shoot, even if that had originally been part of the deal. That was before anyone realized how busy Anthony's would become.

Instead, she fit the shoot into a scheduled day off. It wasn't as if she had a social life, outside of the people she'd met on the job. How could she, when work was all she did?

She arrived for her shoot fifteen minutes early. "Hi! I'm Poppy Springer," she said cheerfully to the young woman at the desk. After being tortured by Dieter and Olga, she was looking forward to the fun part of modeling.

Without looking up, the receptionist gestured toward a collection of mismatched chairs where a nervous teenager sat, accompanied by her mother. "Have a seat over there, and someone will be with you."

She wasn't expecting the red carpet treatment. But she thought they'd at least be waiting for her. Maybe the assistant didn't recognize her. "I'm the new Face of Palette Cosmetics."

"I know who you are. Now if you could just have a seat, someone will be with you shortly."

The teen and her mom had the grace to avert their eyes as Poppy approached them, crestfallen.

An hour later, she was finally led back to a salon chair. The stylist lifted a lock of her hair.

"What products do you use?"

Poppy shrugged. "Just stuff from the drugstore."

She raised a meticulously penciled brow. "I would have liked to have you on a deep-conditioning regimen months ago. Oh well," she sighed, yanking a comb through Poppy's hair. "We'll do the best we can."

After the stylist had washed, conditioned, hacked off three inches, and blown her hair dry, a full-bearded man poked his head in.

"Is she just about ready?" he asked.

"She is. You can have her now."

The stylist whipped off the drape covering Poppy's clothes.

"Call me Flash," said the man, walking Poppy down the hall to a drab, gray-walled space with spindly-legged lights aimed toward a huge roll of white paper suspended from a ceiling beam, unfurled all the way to the floor. In the center of it sat a lonely stool.

"Let's see," said Flash, scraping back hangers on a rolling clothes rack. He withdrew a top. "Try this on. This shade of blue will go well with your coloring."

She went behind a curtain and changed, then took a seat on the stool as directed while Flash went to work adjusting lights and camera angles. He flipped a switch and her hands flew up to shield her eyes from the lights.

"Put your hands down, hon."

She lowered them, self-conscious about where they should go.

"You're stiff as cardboard. How about some tunes?" Without waiting for an answer, Flash blasted some electronic dance music.

He took a few test shots to gauge the lighting. Then he turned on a giant fan and the blades began to whirl.

Poppy's hair flew back from her face in a horizontal sheet. As the fan picked up speed, her neck muscles engaged to keep her head up. While she fought to keep her eyes open, Flash started snapping pictures at a dizzying rate.

"You're squinting," he yelled over the music. "Don't think so hard, honey. You're not being paid to think."

When it was all over, the fan stopped and quiet restored, Poppy's head sagged forward. Her ears rang. She rubbed dry, sandy lids.

"Come over here and look," Flash said, scanning the photos. "You have a real talent for this."

Staggering to her feet, she walked gingerly across the pristine paper, trying not to scuff it, and peered over Flash's shoulder into his camera.

"Those *are* pretty good."

But high cheekbones and the ability to stay seated in a gale didn't mean you were talented. "You're the one who chose the colors. You posed me and adjusted the lights and found the best angles. The credit belongs to you."

Flash looked away from his lens and examined her thoughtfully, in the flesh. "In all the time I've been doing this, I can't remember one girl that ever said that to me. You're a nice person, you know that?"

Poppy smiled—an authentic smile, not a posed one. Now *there* was a compliment she would take.

Flash went back to clicking through proofs, talking to her as he worked. "I get all these girls coming here looking to become famous. Then they find out modeling isn't what they thought it would be. But there's something about you. I saw it in the test shots the Palette people sent over. They saw it, too. Can't put my finger on it, but hey, that's what the pictures are supposed to do, isn't it? Convey what words can't. That's what I was trying to get at when I told you to relax and be yourself."

The real world of modeling might not be very glamorous, but it was a step forward. A step farther away from Clarkston and being a waitress for the rest of her life.

Chapter Twenty-four

Portland couldn't stop raving about Anthony's local and sustainable Northwest fare with its lively bar and wine list highlighting Oregon's best.

Poppy still thought of Heath every day. But by the time she got back to her dark apartment late at night, she was spent, and she knew he'd have been asleep for hours. Then there were those mandatory six a.m. workouts, plus going out to eat on her free nights with Cory or one of the other somms to stay on top of ever-changing trends.

She resisted a growing apprehension that her work might be starting to take over her life. This was what she had wanted, wasn't it? Plus, Cory picked up the tab for all those great meals and good wine. How could she complain?

Groundhog Day came with the prediction of six more weeks of cold and damp. That night before Poppy went home from work, Cory called her into his office.

"How'd you like to take a little break?"

"A vacation?" Her shoulders relaxed. The idea sounded heavenly.

"Just a long weekend away to some place warm." He closed the door behind them. "Our backer whose party you worked Christmas Eve? He's having some people down to his place in Cabo."

Realization set in. "You mean he wants me to work."

"Not this time. As his guest."

"I'm not sure." She might be from the country, but she wasn't that naïve.

Cory read her mind. "It's not like that," he assured her. "It's completely legit. It'll be good for you. Good for business. As you're finding out, people are intrigued by lady somms."

"Who else is going from the restaurant?"

"I am."

At the skeptical look on her face, he brought up a photo on his phone. "Take a look at this. Hard to tell where the infinity pool ends and the Gulf of California begins."

"But . . ."

"The house is huge. You'll have your own bedroom and a private bath."

She still wasn't sure.

"Have you ever flown on a private plane?"

"I've never flown, period," she said sheepishly. "My parents have a motor home. Whenever we go on vacation, we take that."

He pulled up another picture. "Here's the beach."

His snapshots looked like something out of a fancy tourism brochure. Too fancy for the likes of someone who had grown up bussing tables at Poppy's Café in the little town of Clarkston. She couldn't fly off somewhere only to realize she didn't fit in and then be trapped there until the return flight.

"I—I wouldn't even know what to wear."

Cory reached for his wallet and counted out some bills. "Here's a little bonus for you. Get yourself a couple of dresses and a bikini."

Poppy stared at the money in her palm.

"Is this for real?"

"Don't worry." He got up and draped his arm around her casually as he walked her to the door. "I'll take care of you. HR-wise, you're my biggest asset."

The next weekend, when she and Cory walked past everyone shifting their feet in the long security lines to board the sleek little jet sitting on the tarmac, apprehension gave way to excitement.

Inside, the plane reminded Poppy of a narrow living room. There were leather recliners that swiveled and a bar along one side.

Cory helped her off with her jacket. Introductions were made. She jumped when the engines fired up. As they hurtled down the runway faster and faster, she clenched the armrests, held her breath, and watched the ground recede beneath her, leaving the gray-tinged snow and cold behind.

That evening, she was wearing her new, light-as-air dress, sipping fine wine under a tropical sunset.

Cory seemed to know everybody. One by one, he introduced her as his newest sommelier. Their reactions were puzzling. Half treated her like she was one of the servers passing coconut shrimp. The other half tried to impress her by dropping names of vintners they'd met or rare bottles they'd drunk.

The next day she was lying on a lounge, soaking up the hot Mexican sun when Cory spread his towel next to hers.

She tried not to look directly at her boss in his swim trunks.

"Having fun?"

"I can't believe I'm really here."

"This is only the beginning. Wait until your photo spread comes out in May. You're going to be the center of attention everywhere you go. Do you realize that?"

"To tell you the truth, since the shoot ended, I haven't given it another thought."

"Well, you'd better be prepared, because you see this?" He gestured broadly, taking in the pool with its swim-up bar, the villa, and the ocean beyond. "This is just the beginning. Wait and see.

"A few things I want to enlighten you on," he said, slathering on a deliciously scented sunscreen. "Raoul, over there? Real estate broker. You know what they say: location, location, location. So be nice to him. Always good to have someone who knows where the openings are going to be before anyone else does, in case we want to expand. We need him on our side."

"Okay." She had no reason not to be nice to him. To anyone, for that matter.

"And Kelly?"

"The one with the short dark hair who doesn't smile?"

The woman was the epitome of sophistication. Poppy fingered her own long locks absent-mindedly, wondering how she'd look with a pert bob or some chic layers. "I've waited on her."

"Super-smart attorney. We want to keep her well wined and dined. Taking care of her keeps the fees down and the response time short when something goes wrong.

"Last one. Michael."

"The guy in the striped trunks on the diving board." The previous evening sprang to mind, when Michael had held forth on the pool deck, talking loud and long to whoever would listen.

"Cocktail expert at Piper's Pub. You've heard of it?"

She nodded.

"I want him."

Confused, she looked over at Cory. His chest glistened with oil.

"Booze is where our profit margin lies. We've got our wine list on track. Now I want a good cocktail man to help us refine our mixed drinks."

"What do you want me to do?"

"You're good at small talk. Talk to him. Can you swim? Swim up to him. Whatever it takes."

Michael did a cannonball and Poppy shrank at the resulting splash.

And it occurred to her then that though she wasn't in her usual server role, she was still at work.

Two days later, the northbound plane dropped altitude suddenly, leaving Poppy's stomach in her throat. She looked around, but everybody else was still chatting easily.

"Folks," said the pilot over the intercom, "if you're looking out the window, down below you'll see the tiny town of Clarkston. In case you're standing at the bar, time to grab your seat and fasten those seat belts for our descent into the PDX. Local time is six thirty-seven. Temperature is forty degrees under overcast skies."

Clarkston. *Sandy Houser's baby shower!* It was at two o'clock today. Poppy had promised Sandy and Kyle she'd go.

The shower was coed, meaning everyone had been there, women and men. Including Heath.

Poppy's head went back in her recliner. Misgivings flooded through her. She glanced at her newly bronzed arms and realized that as gorgeous as Mexico was, she would rather have spent the weekend catching up with old friends back home than sucking up to some obnoxious guy in hopes that he'd quit his current position and come to work for Cory. Worse, if Michael did come on board, she would be stuck with him on a regular basis.

She peered out the window at the ground rushing toward them and held her breath as the plane bounced down jerkily, followed by a final roar as the engines reversed thrust.

"Hard coming back to forty degrees, isn't it?" asked Cory as they rolled their carry-ons across the tarmac.

He had mistaken her subdued manner for not wanting to come back.

She didn't bother correcting him.

Back in her quiet apartment, she opened her closet door to hang up her jacket. There, on the floor, sat the Housers' baby gift.

What was she going to say to Sandy? *Sorry I was a no-show at your shower, but I was in Mexico with my boss?* Or *Sorry I missed your big event, but I was busy working on my tan?*

And speaking of being tan, she should feel relaxed after spending the weekend in the lap of luxury. Instead, she was drained from trying to draw out people she had nothing in common with, merely to serve her boss's ulterior motives.

Chapter Twenty-five

The winter rains didn't come as often now.

With every passing day, Poppy grew even more proficient at her job, more popular with the dining public.

From the professional women who frequented Anthony's, she observed how to dress well. She bought a few good pieces in subdued colors that she could wear over and over.

Getting up at dawn to endure Dieter's punishing workouts had become routine.

She got six more inches lopped off her hair. Enough to release its natural wave, give it movement.

It turned out she hadn't had to do much prompting to get Michael to come to work for Cory's. He was ready for a move. And yes, his obnoxious voice could be annoying. But he brought in even more business, and that was good for everyone.

Though she'd only been away from home three months, sometimes it seemed like years. She still worked long hours, but she had learned to set boundaries. She no longer felt obligated to spend her one free night checking up on the competition.

One day in early March while she was pulling the cork on a bottle of 2013 Dundee Hills, she felt her phone vibrate.

She checked all her tables and, finding everyone content, went to the wait station and slipped it from her pocket to see a missed call from Junie Hart.

A little flutter of panic set her heart racing. Poppy still wasn't regular at checking social media, but she and Junie stayed in sporadic contact through the occasional text. Calling had gone out of fashion, it seemed. An actual phone call smacked of something out of the ordinary.

She stepped behind a pillar and hit call back.

"Junie? Is everything okay?"

"Everything is better than okay. I'm getting married!"

"You're engaged?!"

To whom? Last she knew, Junie was still pining over a hot-looking ladies' man from back East.

"Manolo. He came back."

"You have a ring?"

"I'm gazing at his grandmother's diamond on my finger right now. I wanted you to hear it from me. And to invite you to my engagement party."

Junie and Manolo's engagement party was more than just a chance for Poppy to toast their happiness. She was still embarrassed over having been a no-show at the Housers' shower.

And it wasn't just the Housers. In such a small town, her disregard for their feelings wasn't likely to have gone unnoticed. She needed to show everyone that her need to prove herself out in the big, wide world didn't take the place of her manners. That she was still the same old Poppy.

She spent her day off shopping for the perfect gift and card. Walking back to her car, she caught a glimpse of her reflection in the window of a clothing store. When had her favorite old jeans become so saggy in the seat? Maybe it was time for a new pair. While she was at it, she let herself be talked into a cute pair of shoes, on sale.

On the night before the engagement party, she set her alarm to give herself plenty of time to get ready and make the drive to Clarkston the next morning. This time she was taking no chances.

The thought of seeing all her oldest and dearest friends was so exciting she could hardly sleep. Especially Junie. If anyone deserved happiness, it was her, after losing first her brother, then her dad, and even her mom when she had moved away to be closer to her work.

There was Sandy, too, with her baby soon coming due. Poppy couldn't wait to see her growing belly.

And of course, her parents. Her heart squeezed at the thought of seeing her mom's smile again, and she couldn't wait to be lifted off her feet in one of Big Pop's giant bear hugs.

And then there was Heath. Adorable, sexy Heath, with the faint worry line between his brows and that wayward lock of hair he was always brushing out of his hazel eyes.

The pause between phone calls had grown longer and longer. And when they did talk, they stuck to safe subjects like work and mutual friends, sidestepping their real feelings.

She hugged Heath's raggedy old dog, burying her nose in it. It still smelled faintly of him, though she feared the smell was fading and might one day be gone forever.

In a few hours, she would see him again. Just imagining his familiar face . . . his reserved yet masculine manner . . . his rock-hard body beneath one of his science guy T-shirts made her insides go all gooey.

She tossed and turned. And then the irony occurred to her: The last time she'd looked forward to something this much was the day she'd left Clarkston to move to Portland.

The next morning, despite leaving in plenty of time, Poppy ran into a traffic tie-up around Tigard. As the minutes wore on, she tapped the steering wheel impatiently. By the time traffic started to flow again, she was fifteen minutes behind schedule.

When she finally reached Broken Hart Vineyards, all the parking spaces close to the building were taken. She parked far away in the grass, gathered up her presents—one for the engaged couple and the other, the belated Houser baby gift—and set out to navigate the uneven ground in her new heels.

The tasting room was abuzz with people. Over the hum, Poppy discerned the voice of her mom in the vicinity of the bar. There she was, sitting next to Red. Poppy headed straight for her.

Red looked up. Wordlessly, she touched Mom's sleeve.

Conversations fell apart as one Clarkstonian after another noted Mom's stunned expression and turned to see what had her mouth agape.

Behind the bar, Sam set down the bottle he'd been pouring from and grinned from ear to ear.

Next to Mom, Big Pop appeared confused at the sight of his very own Poppy.

As for Demi Barnes, talking to Jess over by the window—*well*. If looks could kill, Poppy should be dead.

And then she spied a trim young man with one Western-style boot propped on the bar rail, his only companion a pilsner glass.

A cascade of emotions washed over her, stopping her in the center of the tasting room.

"Heath."

Heath nodded curtly. "Poppy," he replied, in a voice as smooth as good chocolate.

For one pregnant moment, nobody breathed.

Then: "There's my girl!" cried Mom, coming toward her with open arms.

The room exhaled and conversation resumed, to Poppy's great relief.

"Your hair!" Mom exclaimed when she reached her, fingering a shortened lock.

Poppy's best girlfriends gave her mother rein to fawn over her daughter for a few moments before pouncing on her. "What have you done to yourself? You look so . . . grown up!"

Next, Poppy wormed her way toward the bride-to-be.

"I'm so happy you could come," said Junie, embracing her.

"Made Junie's day when you said you could drive down," added Manolo.

Poppy handed Junie her gift. "It took me forever to pick this out. I hope you love it."

"It's from you, isn't it? I know I will," she said, beaming.

"And this one's for you," Poppy told Sandy Houser, standing off to the side, one hand resting atop her very round belly. "I'm so sorry. I feel terrible that I let you down when I didn't come to the shower."

"Pfft." Glowing with the life burgeoning inside her, Sandy waved off her concern. "It's nothing. We're just glad to be seeing you now, on another happy occasion. So how's big-city life? Tell me all about it."

"It's going well." Heath was close. She could feel his presence. Her eyes bounced around the room in search of him, landing instead on one old friend after another. For the most part, she had known them all her life: their strengths, their shortcomings, the unique quirks that made them who they were. "Except for missing all the people back home."

"I'll fill you in. Just tell me what you want to know," said Sandy.

"Everything! Starting with Red and Sam." She nodded to where they stood chatting. "Are they . . . you know. A thing?"

Sandy shrugged. "You see them around together. But there's always a good reason. The fashion show, sometimes at parties. If there's anything more to it than that, they aren't telling. But you've heard Rory's going out with Holly?"

Poppy followed Sandy's eyes over to where Rory had his arm around Holly, talking to a grower.

Where is Heath? She prayed he hadn't left before they had a chance to talk.

"No!"

"He took her to the Valentine's Dance at the Radish Rose."

The Valentine's Dance. *Has that already come and gone?*

A frown caught Poppy's eye from across the room, and her smile faded.

Sandy glanced over her shoulder. "Ah. There's someone who might need a Band-Aid and a happy face sticker."

"I better go talk to him."

She took a deep breath and wound her way through the crowd, returning waves and greetings but determined to reach her destination despite knowing she was in for a tongue-lashing when she got there.

Along the way, bits of surprising news, items of gossip she was no longer privy to reached her ears. She felt oddly isolated. Left out.

"Keval."

"Excuse me. Do we know each other?" Keval stiffened under her embrace.

"You're upset."

"Upset? Why should I be upset? Just because my dear friend disappeared and never texts?"

"I know. I've been terrible."

"Yes, you have been. Speaking of which, how was Mexico?"

Poppy looked around furtively. "I'd appreciate it if you keep that to yourself," she said under her breath. "Sandy would be really hurt if she knew. I didn't intentionally put a trip above Sandy and Kyle. I just forgot."

"Hmph." Keval raised a brow and coolly examined his wine. "And your way of patching the code is to just show up in those shoes—which, by the way are *everything*—and be your old sunny self and all will be forgiven?"

"You're right. I should have called you more. I meant to. I think about you all the time. But I'm just so busy. I work late six nights a week, and then I have to get up early to work out three mornings . . ."

He picked up a cube of Swiss from his plate and held it at shoulder height. "Piece of cheese to go with that whine?" he asked, releasing it into Poppy's hastily cupped hand. "Don't worry. I forgive you."

Something caught his eye. "Oh. Junie's mother is waving to me. I'll be back."

Keval was right. There was no excuse for the way she'd been brushing off the people who still meant so much to her.

Suddenly she reverted to that little girl who needed to be loved unconditionally, regardless of how bad her behavior had been. She looked around for Big Pop and one of his bear hugs and ran smack into Heath, who raised his glass out of the way just in time to avoid sloshing them both with beer.

"Careful."

That voice. If she could only bottle it, take it with her to listen to every time she needed a fix.

The brief touch of his fingers singed her upper arm.

"Sorry." How many apologies did that make in a single day?

A dozen bystanders busied themselves trying to pretend they hadn't witnessed their awkward exchange . . . weren't keeping eyes peeled to see what happened next.

Starved for the sight of him, Poppy let her eyes travel over Heath's body while he rocked on his heels and gazed out Junie's new picture window at the ridged hills that comprised Broken Hart Vineyards.

The design on his tee combined the abbreviations for beryllium and erbium to spell out *BeEr.*

She grasped at something—anything, to bridge the gap that had formed between them over the past months.

"Nice shirt."

"I've heard that line before, somewhere. And I thought *I* was bad at small talk."

"Sorry." *There it is again.*

She tried a different tack. "How's the new brewpub coming along?"

"Huh? Oh." He looked down. "I kind of chucked that idea."

"What? Why? You were so excited about it."

Before he could answer, Junie and Manolo stopped to talk with

Mona Cruz, seated nearby. Manolo slid his arm possessively around Junie's waist. Junie smiled and said something to Manolo, who returned her adoring gaze.

"They look so happy," mused Poppy. "Don't they?"

Pain flashed across Heath's face. He tossed back what was left of his drink. "Need a refill. Nice seeing you."

A dull knife ripped through Poppy's insides. Her nostrils stung with unshed tears.

She looked around again at the people she used to know so well. She might have changed her appearance a little, but on the inside, she was the same old Poppy. But now they were telling new stories—unfamiliar stories about events she hadn't been to and people she'd lost track of. Life in Clarkston was going on without her.

What am I doing here? These were her people. She missed them. She had come to make herself feel better, but in doing so had made some of them feel bad.

Where do I belong?

She wasn't sure anymore.

But she couldn't let Heath go like that. She took off after him.

"Poppy. Wait."

It was Red.

"Think."

"But—" She looked longingly after Heath, just out of reach.

"Do you want to make it worse?"

"What are you talking about?"

"Make up, and then reject him, over and over again?"

She scowled. "I didn't reject Heath. I went to Portland to pursue my passion. It had nothing to do with him." With *us.*

"That's not how he sees it."

Poppy grabbed a glass of champagne from a passing tray and downed half of it. "That's ridiculous."

"Have you forgotten his history?"

Now her anger channeled itself in Heath's defense. "There's nothing wrong with Heath. It's not his fault his mother couldn't deal."

"Of course it's not. But it's human nature to question our own worth just when our self-esteem is hurting most. Remember how much you hated being reminded of that silly senior superlative right after you lost your job at the wine shop?"

Realization began to dawn.

"His brewpub," she reflected, her anger waning. "That's why he stopped progress on it."

Red nodded. "Shortly after you left."

Poppy started toward him again, but again Red reached out to stop her.

"I have to find him! To explain."

"And then what? Walk away again? Who are you trying to make feel better by going after him now? Heath? Or yourself?"

She paused, her chest rising and falling. Her head was a whirl of conflicting emotions, the two sides of her divided in a contest of self-control.

"It's not fair. Every time I go, I hurt Heath. But if I'd stayed, I'd be giving away what I fought so hard for."

"*Life's* not fair. And having choices can be hard. You're my friend. I don't judge, and you don't owe me any explanations. But Heath's my friend, too, and it pains me to see him hurting. All I'm asking is for you to recognize that for every choice you make, there are consequences."

Poppy looked at Heath, alone as usual, his head bowed over his untouched drink, and bit her lip. All their lives, she had considered it her calling to comfort him. And right now, he looked like he'd never needed comforting more.

But as usual, Red was right.

She floundered for something to latch on to, to keep her from hurting him more than she already had. Before she knew what she was doing, her nails dug into Red's soft flesh.

"I can't do this," she said breathlessly.

"It's okay," said Red.

"No, it's not. I have to go."

"Let's go outside on the patio."

"No, I mean I have to leave."

"Come on," said Red maternally, leading her toward the door. "I'll go out with you."

But once they were outside, Poppy kept on going, toward her car.

"When I'm away from him, I can pretend he'll always still be there. That things will never change. But every time I see him, he's like a drug, and I'm an addict. I want him again. It's so intense. And you're right. It's not fair to him."

160 • *Heather Heyford*

At the real risk of twisting an ankle, she forged ahead, her spiky heels sinking into the soft earth with every step.

Red scurried to keep up. "You're feeling fragmented. But self-awareness is the first step to getting a grip on your feelings."

Poppy stopped and faced her friend. "Stop analyzing me! I've got this. I know what I have to do. I just can't come home anymore."

On she marched.

"I respect that," said Red to her back.

Poppy threw up her hands and whirled back around. Her spurt of activity must have helped the blood flow to her head. Clarity was coming back. Or maybe it was just that she was at a remove from Heath, her trigger. At any rate, she became aware of the absurdity of her surroundings, standing out in the middle of a tire-rutted meadow dotted with wood violets in high heels. She squinted. Spending most of the past four months indoors, she'd forgotten how bright the midday sun could be.

"If I do come back, I can't see *him*."

Like the good therapist that she was, Red said nothing, just let the gravity of Poppy's own words sink in.

Around the time Poppy reached her car, it struck her that she was still referring to Clarkston as "home."

Chapter Twenty-six

"Hey."

Heath looked up to see Mona Cruz at his elbow.

Not ten feet away from them, Junie and Manolo accepted yet another offer of good wishes. They smiled into each other's eyes, then kissed.

Heath looked away.

"When you're surrounded by all that gushiness, it's kind of hard not to feel left out, isn't it?" she observed.

In answer, he quietly sipped his ale.

"Are you in love with Poppy?"

Heath jerked his head toward Mona in surprise. "That's a pretty blunt question."

"I'm a blunt person. Saves a lot of time." Her expression was transparent and kind.

He considered. "Love is the most powerful force in the universe. It can't be broken down to the molecular level."

"What's that supposed to mean?" She chuckled, looking askance at him.

"Poppy and I are friends. That's it. There's no romance, no love."

"Good try. But I don't believe a word of it. Let's switch gears. What's this about you starting a brewpub? I wasn't trying to eavesdrop, but I couldn't help overhearing."

"I thought about it. It's the latest trend. But I changed my mind."

"How come? Clarkston needs something like that. This whole town is being overrun by wineaux. If you ask me, it's high time we beer drinkers take a stand. Speaking of, where'd you get that brewski? I've been dying for one."

"You want one?" he asked, signaling the bartender. "It's all brought in from my brewery for the party."

"Is that right? What do you recommend?"

"Give her a Newberg Neutral," he told the bartender.

"I've always preferred craft beer to wine. A bit of a hophead, if you want to know the truth."

"That so?"

"It's not just the beer, it's the culture. You know what they say: 'Beer people are good people.' I found that out when I was living down in California. Everyone from the brewer to the distributor to the bartender is nice, and interesting, and often, funny."

Heath turned toward her, drawn by their common interest.

"What's your favorite?"

She laughed and held up her glass, examining the golden brew. "Whatever I'm drinking at the time. Except for that mass-produced stuff I call 'beer water.' Seems like every time I visit a new brewery and meet the staff, I leave with a new favorite. Craft brewers care about the product, plus they're super welcoming. They put their hearts and souls into what they make. But, hey, who am I telling? You know that."

"I know about the production end . . ."

She cocked her head, as if waiting for him to finish. "Yeah?"

Dare I say what I'm thinking? He'd had just enough beers to do it. "What I'm missing is the welcoming gene."

"Well, all you need is someone to do that part for you."

"That's the problem," he said, going back to his drink. "You just hit the nail on the head."

"Why not me?" she chirped.

He swung his head back to her. "You?"

"Sure! I used to tend bar. I'm a walking proponent of craft beer. I know that it is better for you than red wine. It has more nutrients and fiber and antioxidants. Craft beer may have more calories and higher alcohol than the regular kind, but because it's more flavorful, you drink less of it. What with all the different styles plus the seasonal brews, you can drink something different every time."

Heath scratched his chin.

"Plus, if you haven't heard, I need a job."

He studied her. "How long you been back in town?"

"Six months. I'm through looking for something else, somewhere else. I found out that whatever it was I was looking for couldn't be found on the outside."

"And what was that?"

"Self-acceptance." She tapped her chest. "Turned out it was right in there, all along."

Daryl Decaprio sauntered up on Mona's other side and started talking to her.

She certainly was outgoing, almost as much as Poppy. And with her enthusiasm for the subject, she'd be perfect for a brewpub's front-of-house. That is, if he were looking for someone.

After a moment, she climbed off her stool. "Thanks for the beer!" she said cheerfully. "See you around!"

Chapter Twenty-seven

After her disastrous trip home to Junie and Manolo's party, Poppy realized that while her professional life might be skyrocketing, her personal life kind of stunk.

The only friends she'd made—if you could call them that—were her coworkers at Anthony's. And the only thing they had in common was their job. Morgan kept his personal life private, and Stu, understandably, spent all his free time with his wife and baby son.

Most of the servers were from the city and already had full social lives.

She had more invitations to restaurant openings and art exhibits and charity events than she could handle. But nothing lasting had come out of them.

Was it any wonder she was lonely? That she didn't yet feel like she belonged in Portland?

It didn't help that she worked the very hours that most other people her age were out and about.

Back home, her café clientele represented a cross section of the tiny town, from the growers at the farmer's market whom they bought their produce from to the banker who held their mortgage and everyone in between. Regulars were just that—they showed up often, some on a daily basis. Not only did they like to pass the time of day with the Springers, they talked to each other, too, craning their necks over the booths to add their two cents to an overheard conversation, getting up from the counter to sit for a spell with neighbors at a nearby table or just to have a cup of coffee and shoot the breeze.

Anthony's patrons came from all corners of the city, the state, and even beyond. They tended to either be in awe of Poppy in her position as a rare female sommelier or not know the difference between her and the food servers.

And then there were the useful associates Cory cultivated like charms on a bracelet.

Late one April evening, Cory introduced her to a well-dressed man dining alone in the evening's final seating.

"Poppy Springer, I'd like you to meet Simon Matthews."

The man looked Poppy over with frank appreciation. "So, this is the lovely new lady somm I've been hearing so much about," he quipped in a British accent. His manicured hand reached for hers and held it for a fraction of a second longer than was necessary.

"You've heard of Simon. The syndicated wine columnist from London? He's on a tour of the American wine country."

As in, print? Poppy could hardly let on that she never read anything longer than a few sentences, and that, on her phone.

If you haven't, pretend you have was the message in Cory's eyes.

"Oh! Yes! So nice to meet you, Mr. Matthews."

A waiter appeared at Cory's elbow, looking stressed. "When you're finished, can I have you for a minute?"

Cory looked pulled in two directions. "Poppy will take good care of you," he assured Simon before leaving to put out whatever fire had erupted.

"I have no doubt," said the man, with a gleam in his eye.

Following some pleasant chitchat and a look at the menu, Mr. Matthews unblinkingly accepted her suggestion on the best wine to pair with his meal. The appetizer and entrée went off without a hitch. Now, as she was pouring his third glass, he smiled and said, "Your shift is almost finished, is it not?"

She glanced around the room at her few remaining tables. There would be no more wine ordered tonight.

"Almost."

"You must have been on your feet for ages. Care to sit down for a bit?"

He smelled pleasantly like lavender and leather, and although she guessed his age to be only mid-thirties, he looked like he probably had a valet waiting for him back in jolly olde England.

Despite his undeniable swoon-worthiness, Poppy searched for a tactful way to explain that sommeliers did not sit down with diners.

But over at the hostess station, Cory caught her eye. He gave her a nod so small she might have imagined it.

"Do, please." Simon pulled out the seat next to him.

"Well. Okay, for a minute."

"Tell me about yourself."

She gave him her little spiel about the wine shop and how she was basically self-taught.

"Amazing. You and I have much in common. I am largely self-taught, as well. You see, I have a condition in which letters and numbers appear all topsy-turvy. Quite problematic at times. Couldn't make heads nor tails of it until way after the other lads, I'm afraid."

Poppy's eyes grew wide. "You have—dyslexia?"

"Sorry." He smiled endearingly. "Do you think you can overlook my shortcoming? Because I should be *devastated* if it should in any way interfere with our budding friendship."

"No—I—" Poppy stuttered.

"Sorted it out on my own, eventually. Had to, so I could fulfill my dream of becoming a writer. Hard to make those who haven't experienced a learning disability understand."

"Oh, but I do!" she said. "I have dyslexia, too!"

"You don't say? Quite the coincidence. Well then, it appears we have more than just wine in common."

They talked until closing. Once, she excused herself to tend to her tables, but Cory came over and told her he would see to it.

Afterward, she let Simon walk her down the street where Cory wouldn't be, as Simon said, "looking over their shoulders," and buy her a nightcap.

"It's been lovely to meet you, Poppy. I'm leaving tomorrow for California and points south, but I'll be back in a week. I'll let you in on a secret, if you'll promise not to tell. Not even your boss."

"I promise."

"It's true that I'm here on assignment. But I'm also contemplating a move. I'm interviewing for a position with a wine association here in Oregon."

"Really?"

"I'm taking a month off to explore the area. It would be lovely to have a tour guide with your extensive knowledge of the local terroir."

It took her a second to realize he meant *her*.

Well, she had an easy out. "I'd like to help you, but we're so busy around here . . ."

"I've known Cory for years. I could put in a word." He gave her a meaningful look as he sipped his wine.

A little wave of panic stirred in Poppy. *What about Heath?*

"You seem a bit reluctant. Have I overstepped? Are you spoken for?"

Am I? She didn't know. This was the first time the question had come up since she moved.

"It's . . . complicated."

Simon took her indecisiveness in stride. "There's no hurry. Think about it, and I'll ring you up when I'm back this way. Sound good?"

"Sure. Sounds good." What else could she say?

Chapter Twenty-eight

That night in bed, Poppy hugged Heath's dog tight.

Customers had flirted with her before. But she'd never been tempted. And yet sooner or later, she was bound to meet someone she was attracted to.

Who wouldn't be tempted by the likes of Simon Matthews? He was confident, charming, and successful. And wonder of all wonders, he knew firsthand what it felt like to have been born with a learning disability—and to have successfully battled it.

It was possible that nothing would come of his job interview. But it wasn't the prospect of starting a long-term relationship that bothered her. It was not knowing where exactly things stood with her and Heath.

Maybe she was making too big a deal out of this. She could go out with Simon, and Heath might never know.

But *she* would.

Poppy's female coworkers pounced on her the day after Simon Matthews had made his appearance. Word had gotten around that Cory had finished up her shift for her and they'd been seen leaving together.

Poppy tried to downplay the whole thing, but it wasn't easy when she was being peppered with questions and told how lucky she was to have been singled out by such a hot guy.

Days later, they were still talking about it.

She needed to touch base with something solid and real and familiar, to get her bearings, before she gave Simon her decision.

On her next day off, she rose at dawn, as usual. But this time, instead of subjecting herself to Dieter's punishing lunges and curls, she canceled her workout and headed south.

It had been four months since she'd left Clarkston, but her Mini seemed to know the way by itself. This morning, virtually every traffic light she hit glowed green. It seemed like a sign.

Between the bedroom community of Sherwood and Newberg, the first towns on the edge of wine country, subtle signs of spring caught Poppy's eye. The blossoms of an Oregon grape flashing yellow amidst the brown scrub awakened her city-numbed senses. She noticed fuzzy willow catkins lining the road. Robins congregating in the pastures where here and there, horses had been let out to graze the pale new grass.

When she reached Clarkston, she had a rogue urge to park on Main Street and enter the café through the front door instead of going through the kitchen like she always used to do. Now that she no longer worked there, she wanted to view Poppy's from a different perspective, as a customer, not someone who had grown up there.

The familiar cinnamon scent of Mom's sticky buns warmed her heart.

"Hey! Look who's here!" Grinning from ear to ear, Big Pop came out from behind the counter and smothered her to his chest.

She felt infinitely better already.

Mom was waiting her turn. "Honey! I didn't know you were coming! Is everything okay?"

"Everything's fine. Can't I visit my parents on my day off?"

"Well, sure," she said, wringing her hands. "It's just that . . . you came unannounced. We weren't exactly ready for you."

"What's there to get ready?"

But before Mom could answer, all over the café, hands went up in greeting.

It took her a full fifteen minutes to circulate the room, swapping news with everyone who demanded her attention. As she talked and listened, she looked around, comparing the appearance of her humble namesake café with the upscale establishment where she now worked.

There was no comparison. While Anthony's had dark paneled walls and mahogany tables clothed in white linen, the café had red vinyl booths and metal-legged tables topped with Formica.

She glanced up at the chalkboard menu on the wall. Turkey BLTs hardly measured up to thirty-six-dollar-a-plate halibut cheeks.

"So, what do you think about that?" The president of the Clarkston Savings Bank, a lanky, silver-haired man in jeans and neatly tucked flannel shirt, jerked his thumb in the direction of the picture window.

Poppy hadn't noticed the rectangular sign propped against the glass, facing outward. Some sixth sense made her stomach drop.

Part of her didn't want to take a closer look. But another, perverse part propelled her feet forward.

Mom stepped in front of her. "Let's sit down and talk first. It's been so long since we had a little heart-to-heart."

"Let her go, Scarlett," said her father. "She has to find out sometime."

Reluctantly, Mom stepped to the side.

There, her worst fear was confirmed.

She picked up the sign and carried it over to where her parents stood.

"Why?"

"Well, honey, we're getting older, that's why." She twisted her dish towel. "There's a lot we haven't been able to do. Traveling, for instance. We've never been to the southwest, and you know we've always wanted to go."

"We got that big motor home just sitting out there in the drive. And now that I'm eligible for Social Security—"

"And you've established yourself somewhere else," Mom reminded her.

"We just listed it this week. We thought we had plenty of time to tell you. But wouldn't you know, we already got a bite."

"Might as well tell you all of it," said Mom, looking up anxiously at Big Pop. "We put the house on the market, too."

Poppy steadied herself with a hand on a nearby table.

"No sense in hanging on to it when we're going to be living in the motor home."

The thought of her house and the café not being there was inconceivable. Those strong, steady roots were what had given her the strength to branch out.

"You look a little shaky. Come sit down," said Mom.

Poppy did as she was told.

"How are you? How's your job?"

How could Mom expect her to answer her inane questions, after the bombshell she'd just dropped?

"Fine," she said, in a daze.

She continued to mouth pat answers to Mom's queries, too stunned to do anything else.

"Are you planning to go over to Heath's while you're here?"

At the sound of his name, Poppy blinked. After the engagement party, she had determined that it was best for Heath if she stayed away. But now she needed him like never before.

"Won't do no good." A grower from the market turned around and slung his elbow over the upholstered back of the booth. "He's not home."

"Where is he?" Poppy heard herself ask.

"Prob'ly still not done moving his dad over to Liz Greenburn's place. They started yesterday. But you know his dad's got a lot of stuff to move."

The two women eating sticky buns at the counter swung around as one. "Scott Sinclair is moving in with Liz Greenburn?" they asked in tandem.

"That's right," said the man, reveling in being the bearer of juicy gossip.

"The caterer?" Poppy interjected.

"Yep. Nobody saw that coming. Almost twenty years Scott's been alone. I hear he'd become somewhat of a recluse. Some say even a hoarder. Then Liz got ahold of him, turned him around right quick."

So many changes. What would Heath do without having to check on his dad every day? On the one hand, it was a blessing. But on the other . . . whom else did Heath have?

She slid out of the booth.

"Where are you going?" asked Mom.

"To Heath's."

"Have something to eat first."

"I—I couldn't eat."

"Will you be back?"

"I don't know."

Chapter Twenty-nine

Not long after talking to Mona at the engagement party, Heath had called up his marketing manager and told him he would be accompanying him to the next Brewer's Guild meeting.

"Are you serious?"

"I'm serious."

"I've been begging you to do this for the past year, and it's been like bangin' my head against a wall. I gotta know. What changed your mind?"

What was the final straw? Was it that a certain caterer had done what no one had been able to do in twenty years—capture his dad's broken heart, lightening Heath's load?

Or that the love of Heath's life had chosen fame and notoriety over him?

Maybe it was Mona Cruz, showing up at the point when he'd hit rock bottom, like some brewing angel of mercy.

Or maybe it was all three of those things.

"It's not important," said Heath, when really, *nothing* could be more important.

"Whatever. I'm just glad you're finally coming around."

"I'm only going to a meeting, not making any promises."

"I'll take what I can get."

Heath had no way of knowing that that day would prove to be life-changing. At that meeting of brewers, he would discover a like-minded group of bright men and women who were committed to the highest level of their craft. In short, he would finally find his tribe.

The whole way home, he wouldn't be able to stop talking about the ideas he'd heard and how he planned to put his personal spin on them.

John would be ecstatic, and so would the rest of the team, when he told them that they were going to do it—that they were going to finally have their brewpub.

Chapter Thirty

Poppy slowed her Mini to a crawl when she passed Heath's old house, the one he'd grown up in. In the front yard she saw a huge pile of junk. Furniture, old rugs, toys...more stuff than a ranch house that size could conceivably contain. The windows were bare of curtains. There was no sign of either Heath's car or his dad's.

Picking up speed, she drove on several hundred yards until she came to Heath's new place.

Parked next to his car was another, unfamiliar one.

Poppy pulled in behind Heath and got out. When she walked by the strange vehicle, the sight of a child's booster seat in the back puzzled her.

Who among their friends had a kid that age?

She rang the doorbell once. Twice.

Then she heard the faint sound of children's voices coming from behind the house.

She made her way around to the path that led down to the creek.

The scent of a lilac bush in bloom brought back a fond memory of a necklace Heath had given her the Saturday after she'd flunked yet another math test. Only with a backward glance did she notice that that little bush had grown along with her, until today it was as tall as she was.

The voices grew louder. Were these kids from the strange car parked next to Heath's? Some new people in the area? Or out-of-state visitors run amok? Tourists had been known to carry their picnic baskets right out into people's vineyards, without asking permission.

But there weren't any vineyards out back here, just the woods and the Chehalem.

Her old protectiveness toward Heath sprang to the forefront. He wouldn't be happy when he found out his privacy had been invaded.

Once she got to a certain spot, it wouldn't be hard to see through the branches to the tree house and its surroundings. The oaks and maples wouldn't fully leaf out until May.

When she reached the clearing, she slowed her steps and peered below.

Two of the Adirondack chairs had been moved side by side. Dappled sunlight played across the features of Heath and—

Mona Cruz?

Poppy blinked.

At Heath's feet lay his dozing dogs, their fur wet and matted from a dip in the creek.

Two skinny young boys, one of them armed with a big stick, poked around in the brush.

"Can we swing on this, Heath?" called the smaller of the two, pointing to where the frayed rope hung from a high branch over a deep pool.

They must know him pretty well to be using his first name.

"Not that one. It's too old. Maybe this summer I'll replace it, and then I'll show you how we used to swing out."

How *they* used to swing out. Heath and Poppy and a very select group of others. This was *their* place. Or used to be.

Seconds ticked by while Poppy struggled to make sense of what she was looking at.

By the looks of things, he and Mona sure had a lot to talk about. Heath was going on with rare abandon.

A minute passed, and still she couldn't tear her eyes off the scene of tranquil domesticity. Heath sat forward on the edge of his seat, legs spread, elbows propped on his knees, geek tee rippling across flat abs when he raised his arms to make a point.

Mona, wearing a short romper affair, slouched sideways facing him, a foot tucked beneath her.

But Poppy could only make out what they said when Heath raised his voice to warn the smaller boy away from the bank, or Mona yelled at the older one to stop running with the stick.

So, this was how Heath had chosen to occupy himself now that she had gone away and his dad had moved in with his girlfriend. And to think of all the time she'd wasted worrying about him! It hadn't taken long for him to find solace. No wonder, though, with Mona moving in on him the minute the competition was out of sight. A guy like Heath didn't have a chance.

She was almost sick with jealousy. Thank God she had happened by when she did! If not, how long would it have been before she found out about them? When would Heath have told her?

Not that she called him much anymore, a small inner voice reminded her.

Well, those two could have each other!

Once she'd made up her mind she wasn't going down there to confront them, she became terrified that they would spot her spying on them.

She began gingerly backing up the hill one step every time, praying that she wouldn't snap a twig or fall and give herself away. But she didn't get far before one of those wild-child boys came tearing up the path in her direction.

The grade was steep, forcing him to slow down, bow his head, and use his tree limb as a walking stick.

He was coming right at her. She could hear him panting with exertion.

She looked frantically at Heath and Mona, but in their deep connection to each other, they were oblivious. What could she do? She couldn't retreat now without drawing attention to herself. She was trapped.

The boy halted when he saw her sandals in the center of the path, mere inches away. His eyes climbed up her body to meet hers.

She put her finger to her lips. "Shhhh!" she hissed, in a last-ditch attempt to remain hidden.

There was a second's pause before he threw back his head and opened his mouth so wide Poppy could see his uvula dangling in the back of his throat. Then he screamed a bloodcurdling, *"Moooooom! Stranger danger!"*

At the sound of Miguel's shriek, Heath was on his feet in an instant. But he only stumbled a few steps forward before he saw Miguel face-to-face with—*Poppy?*

He froze, confused. She was supposed to be in Portland.

Meanwhile, Mona had downshifted into full mama-bear mode. She was already halfway to Miguel.

"Poppy!" She doubled over with relief when she saw her, her hand to her chest. "Thank God. It's only you."

She turned on her son. "What are you doing, screaming like that, scaring me out of my wits, eh? I should take that stick of yours and swat you with it."

Miguel frowned and pointed an accusing finger at Poppy. "She scared me!"

"That's Poppy Springer. She's nothing to be scared of."

Mona grinned at Poppy. "I don't know what came over him. What are you doing here?" She brushed a jet-black curl out of her eyes. "I didn't know you were back in town."

Poppy jammed her fists on her hips, straightened to her full height, and peered down her nose at Mona. "What are *you* doing here?"

"Me?" Mona tossed her head over to where Heath stood, watching warily. "Me and Heath are talking about business."

"Business?" Poppy raised a doubtful brow.

Mona's grin disappeared. "Yes," she replied, thrusting out her impressive chest in self-defense. "Business. Is that a problem?"

Mona had never been the type to back down from a fight.

"What kind of business?" As she asked it, she looked over Mona's head at Heath.

Mona looked back at him, too. "You tell her," she said. "I think it's your place.

"Manuel!" she yelled. "Come on. We're leaving."

"Aw, Mom! Do we have to?"

"I said, get over here. Time to go."

"You don't have to—" Heath sputtered.

"Yes, we do. You two have things to talk about," Mona said, tossing Poppy a significant look.

"We'll touch base later," Heath called.

Heath watched Mona herd her children up the path, leaving him and Poppy alone by the creek, just like in old times.

"What the hell?" Poppy said with a flick of her hand. "What am I supposed to think when I come walking over the hill and I find you and Mona all cozied up here like two . . . lovebirds?"

"*Lovebirds?* We were talking about beer."

"Ha! She said you were talking about business."

"We were. The *beer* business."

"I knew something was up the minute I saw you together."

"Nothing is up. But what if there was? I didn't know I was tethered to you."

"Teth—?" She actually stomped her foot.

"Tethered. You got a better word?"

"We. Are. Not. Tethered. We aren't—anything." Poppy huffed, her jaw tense.

"What about you? What are *you* doing here?"

"I came here to see if there was anything between us. Anything salvageable. Guess I know the answer to that now."

She whirled around and headed back up the path.

"Poppy, come back here. You've got it all wrong."

To his relief, she stopped and turned. "Do I?"

"Yes, you do. But even if there was something going on between Mona and me, who could blame me? *You* left *me*, remember?"

"I didn't *leave* you!" she said with a grimace. "I went to find myself! There's a big difference!"

"Really?" Heath saw red. "And what's that? You had everything." He flung his arms wide. Spittle flew from his mouth as he went on. "You're beloved in this town. What more could you want?"

"Self-respect! That's what! But how would you know about that? You never had to struggle with learning something as simple as the alphabet! You never flunked a whole grade! Nobody wrote trash about you in the yearbook!"

She stomped a few steps and then turned around expectantly. "Well? I drove all the way down here to see you. Aren't you even going to walk me to my car?"

She made no sense. The woman drove him crazy.

"Why should I? Like you said, we aren't 'anything.'"

With a sniff, she stormed off at double time.

Behind her back, he stared at the exaggerated sway of her ass, as elegant as a mathematical proof—succinct, surprising, and innovative.

Chapter Thirty-one

Poppy's Palette ad campaign was launching at the end of May. In preparation, the local press and a handful of restaurant industry publications interviewed her.

A week before the launch, Cory called Poppy into his office.

"I'm loving all this press," he said, genuinely caught up in the excitement of the launch. "This is a big day for us. Six months in business, our very own Poppy in a major ad campaign. Things are good."

Poppy smiled under his praise. She had worked hard.

"I'm raising your pay twenty-five percent."

Her mouth fell open. "That is . . . more than generous."

"You deserve it. Annnnd . . . I say it's time for a celebration. I'm throwing a release party in your honor. I've made the arrangements myself. All the RSVPs are in."

"What?"

"The week of Memorial Day will be slow. We'll have it that Tuesday. Six o'clock, the private banquet room. All the top Palette execs will be there. The photographer. Then there's Kelly, our attorney, Raoul, the Realtor, some bloggers. The mayor said he'd try to stop by, schedule permitting. And Simon Matthews will be in town."

Poppy had gone for drinks with Simon twice since her big fight with Heath, but nothing more. She had returned to Portland more determined than ever to make things work. What choice did she have? Heath had moved on. With the café closing at the end of the month and spring the ideal time for a house to be on the market, it would only be a matter of time before that was gone, too. There was nothing to go back to.

She stuffed her feelings into a box along with Heath's old, threadbare dog and stuck it in the back of her closet where she wouldn't be reminded of him.

But she didn't want to cut *all* her ties.

"I promised I'd be home that day. A bunch of us always go on a hike. We've been doing it since we were teenagers."

It was a whole-day affair, starting out with the strenuous hike in the hills of the Coast Range, followed by a cookout. In the evening, they rented the community pool where Poppy and Junie used to work as lifeguards.

"Take the following couple of days off. People will be staying home to grill. It'll be dead around here. As far as the menu, we're going to do mozzarella toasts with herb oil, a creamy tofu and green pea dip . . ."

But Poppy was thinking longingly of hot dogs and hamburgers done on a park grill.

Then she had an idea. "Can I ask you something?"

"Whatever you want. You're my star employee."

"Can I invite a few of my own guests? My parents would be beyond thrilled to be a part of it. And there are a couple of special friends I'd like to include, too . . ."

"The guest list is already set." He shifted in his seat. "You have to understand," he said, looking vaguely annoyed. "This is all for publicity for the restaurant. That's the bottom line. It's coming out of my marketing budget."

When Cory had said he was having a party in her honor, she'd naturally assumed there would be people there that meant something to her. Not the usual crowd he kept placated with favors so that if he ever needed them, they'd be obligated to come running.

She couldn't help but compare Cory's event to the impromptu going-away party Heath had held for her the night of the reunion, to celebrate her passing her test. Heath didn't even like parties, but he had opened up his brand-new, gorgeous home on the spur of the moment for her, and included every single person at the reunion.

On the day of her party, Cory showed up wearing a new suit. He had had a special backdrop created with all of his restaurant names plastered across it, and he pressed Flash, her Palette photographer, into service, posing with Poppy in a dozen ways for use across all his PR platforms.

That explains poor Flash's presence, thought Poppy. *It's a working party for him, too.*

Cory's arm drew her in tighter to his side and Flash's camera whirred. Then, one by one, Cory corralled his VIP guests toward the backdrop, where they were more than happy to pose with his "star employee." In fact, thought Poppy as she smiled and said "cheese" yet again, the photo op seemed to be the main reason for the get-together.

Simon was the one light in the crowd. He took her hand in his and kissed both cheeks.

"I knew you were garnering a bit of a following as a sommelier, but I had no idea you modeled, too," he said in his crisp accent.

"I don't, really," she replied. "This is my first time."

"The photos are lovely. You're quite multitalented."

"Thanks, Simon." She looked around to make sure no one overheard, and asked, "How's the job prospect coming along?"

"Very well, actually. Seems it's down to two candidates. Oddly enough, I seem to be one of them."

"That's not odd at all. It's great. I'm really happy for you."

"I am as well. But not just because of the job. There's a lovely American I wouldn't mind seeing more of."

Poppy hesitated. Simon was really nice, and they could talk wine for hours. But when he held her hand, she felt . . . nothing.

"You should know something. I want to take things slow. I hope I haven't been leading you on."

"Not at all. I'm not a rube. I can tell there's something unresolved that you're dealing with. And when you do, I'd like to be here, waiting."

Poppy smiled politely, but her mouth ached from grinning and her feet hurt. At work, she wore clogs, and she was so busy moving around she didn't even notice it. This evening she'd been standing around in four-inch heels with nothing to do but accept obligatory congratulations and make watery small talk.

Feeling hollow, she thought of Junie and Red and Sam and all her other friends back home, enjoying each other's company. And of Heath, with Mona playing the role of chatty foil that Poppy had always owned.

Her relief was palpable as she watched Cory walk the last guest to the door and shake his hand good-bye. Alone, she exited the kitchen into the alley, peeled off her heels, and limped to her car.

* * *

Red called Poppy later that night.

"Can you spare a minute to chat?"

"Of course."

"I don't want to bother you. I know you have important things to do."

Has it come to this—the people I care for most reduced to begging for a morsel of my time? "You could never bother me."

"We missed you at the hike."

"I missed you, too. Sorry I had to work." Nobody in Clarkston would consider that party "work," but she knew better.

"One of us, in particular."

Awkward pause.

"Heath and I are through."

"What makes you say that?"

"I saw him and Mona Cruz down by the creek surrounded by his dogs and her boys."

"And?"

"They were cozied up in the Adirondack chairs with her kids running around like it was their second home."

"I—" Red stuttered—a totally foreign sound, coming from Clarkston's Best Therapist. "I'm pretty sure that was nothing."

"Really?" *Funny. That's what Heath said.* "Because it sure looked like the cover of next year's Christmas card to me."

A relieved laugh burst through the phone. "You know about the new brewpub, right?"

"Heath was going to open one, but then he quit." She didn't add *at the same time I left town.* She already felt bad enough about her role in tanking that project.

"It seems as though he's resurrected the idea. I drove by his operation the other day and noticed that it's under construction. Sam told me he's adding on a space in the front where people can come and drink his beers on tap, and Mona's going to work there."

Brassy, sassy Mona. With her big personality, she'd be great in the front of the house.

She couldn't hate Mona for that. Hadn't she been Heath's first choice for the job, and turned him down?

But she still wasn't convinced there wasn't more going on between Mona and Heath than just work.

She hung up reluctantly, wondering how her life had gotten so out of whack. Then she changed into her old flannel pajamas and got on-line to see if pictures from the hike had been posted yet . . . as if her mental pictures weren't torture enough.

Her heart flooded with warmth and longing when she saw the achingly familiar silhouettes backlit by an orange sunset, clowning around in their shorts and sneakers.

Unlike her at her party, they looked like they were having a blast.

There was Keval's smirk. Red's open-mouthed profile, about to bite into her hot dog. Junie and Manolo, glued at the hip.

And the one she was really looking for—Heath. But instead of the picture she'd dreaded, of Mona hanging on him, he was sitting by himself holding a stick threaded with marshmallows, contemplating the campfire.

Poppy went to her closet, pulled out the shoe box in the back, and sat down on the edge of her bed.

She opened the lid and stared at Heath's old dog.

And then she took it out, lay down, turned off her new lamp, and just held the token of him close, breathing in the comforting smell of green woods and leather and laundry soap.

Six months into her move, and she realized: *I'm not happy.*

She missed Heath's charming shyness, his dorky tees. The way he always came through for her when she needed something, even when it was at his own expense.

She needed him in her bed, where all of his tentativeness disappeared and he moved with certainty. She loved having that secret side of him. The thought of him sharing it with another woman was almost more than she could bear.

Maybe she had jumped the gun that day she saw him down on the creek. Maybe he was telling the truth—that there really wasn't anything between him and Mona.

Impulsively, she reached for her phone on her bedside table and poised her fingertip above his name.

Then she remembered Red's sage advice—that playing tug-of-war with his heart was selfish. Even cruel.

With resignation, she put back the phone and hugged Heath's dog until she fell asleep.

Chapter Thirty-two

It was the first time in six months that Poppy had two whole days' vacation in a row. She wasn't sure how she was going to spend them, but she had an idea.

She threw some things into a bag and headed back to Clarkston, already savoring a sticky bun for her breakfast.

She cranked up the music and allowed her mind to be a blank the whole way through Tigard, and on through Sherwood and Newberg. But when she reached Clarkston's Main Street, she drove straight past the café, barely getting a glimpse through the big picture windows, and turned right onto North Yamhill.

From a block away from Clarkston Craft Ales, she could see the imposing orange construction vehicles. As she drew closer, she saw the new façade that, according to Red, was going to be Heath's new brewpub.

Before she could change her mind, she parked at a safe distance from the machinery.

It was a warm morning. In the back of the building where the canning took place, the garage door was open.

Poppy looked around at the enormous silver tanks with a bewildering array of gauges and yards of hoses looped around the latches.

The faintly familiar woman working with the canning machine close to the doorway spared her a questioning look.

"Can you tell me where to find Heath?" yelled Poppy over the mechanical din.

"Should be in his office." She nodded toward an inner door.

Heath had given Poppy and some others a group tour of the manufacturing part of the brewery years ago, but she'd never been in the administrative offices. She wandered hesitantly through the hallway, feeling like an intruder.

What did she think she was doing? Her coming here wasn't good for Heath. And not just because she was interrupting him at his job.

She heard voices coming from an open door and peeked inside.

Heath looked up from his chair, facing the door.

John twisted around in his. "Hey, Poppy!" he said courteously, though with a look of puzzlement.

Heath was on his feet. "Is something wrong?"

No wonder he would think that, what with her showing up at his work on a weekday morning. She knew she shouldn't have come.

"No, nothing's wrong," she hastened to put his mind at ease. "I just thought I'd stop by."

Heath released a held breath and dropped his head with obvious relief.

Poppy's nerves felt like a rubber band, stretched to the breaking point. She bit her lip.

For a tense moment, nobody knew what to do, how to act.

"I was just leaving," John lied cheerfully. "Heath, I'll get back to you on that new pressure vessel."

Poppy stepped sideways to let John pass.

He gave her a nervous wave, barely meeting her eyes. "Nice seeing you again, Poppy."

Heath walked around Poppy, shut his door, and glared at her. "What are you doing?"

Poppy looked down. "I know. I shouldn't have come. But I . . . I . . . ."

To her dismay, she started to cry.

In an instant, the defensive atmosphere between them dissolved. A strong arm curled around her, and she realized that, right or wrong, that was what she had come here for.

She turned into him, as naturally as day follows night.

"Don't you ever hesitate to come to me," Heath said low in his throat, in that unvarnished way that she had missed so much.

Poppy was brimming with needless explanations and unnecessary apologies.

". . . then, the next morning when I saw the pictures plastered all over social media, it was written all over my face exactly how miserable I was, I had been, for so very long. The irony was just too much . . ."

"I know," said Heath, stroking her hair.

". . . whole thing was so superficial. Cory, in his new suit with his arm so tight around my waist got me almost wondering if he wanted to make people think he and I were actually a thing . . ."

"But you're not."

"No! Never. And that's when I realized that that was how this whole thing started—as a quest to prove to myself that I was more than just a prom queen . . ."

"Shhhhh," said Heath. Then again, best to get it all out now, because when he got her into his bed, he wanted her head clear of all that old garbage.

". . . Christmas Eve with my family and you and your dad. Sandy and Kyle's baby shower. And then, yesterday, missing the hike . . ."

"I know. It wasn't the same without you."

". . . and worst of all, I'd wasted all that time trying to prove to myself that I was good enough, when I could have been spending that time with you . . ."

He let her sob until all the doubts and misgivings of the past year had been washed away with her tears.

Finally, he raised the hem of his shirt, which read WHEN LIFE HANDS YOU LEMONS, USE THEM TO MAKE CRUDE ELECTROCHEMICAL BATTERIES and used it to mop Poppy's face.

"You okay?" he asked, looking down at her with kindly concern.

She nodded, red-faced and shaky.

"Come on. I'm going to walk you over to a side door, then get the car and pull around and pick you up. Spare us from the gossip mill."

Minutes later, Heath couldn't stop glancing over at the now-subdued Poppy, sitting next to him in his car. He'd missed the heavenly scent of her. Now he took full advantage of her proximity, breathing her in with slow inhalations.

He'd been longing for this moment without knowing if or when it would come, or what it would look like when it did. It didn't matter anymore. All that mattered was that it was finally here. She was home.

When they got to his house he took her hand and led her down the steep path, across the forest floor, and up the ladder to the tree house, neither of them speaking.

He rolled his bed with the purple comforter and the casters he had nailed onto it out onto the outdoor platform.

Then he went back to her and started methodically unbuttoning her shirt. He slipped the sleeves off her shoulders.

In silence, he unbuckled her sandals and lifted first one of her feet and then the other, and then he unzipped her pants and she stepped out of those, too.

Heath's need for release was so long overdue he wasn't sure he could make it. He pulled his shirt over his head, slipped out of his jeans, and stood in front of her.

Then he did something he'd wanted to do since the day he'd watched the exaggerated sway of her posterior as she'd stalked off in a fit of temper after seeing him with Mona. He reached around and cupped that fine ass and drew her hips into his.

"Oh," she said, her eyes flying open.

He looked down at her lashes, pale as straw. He watched her sapphire eyes begin to glow at the feel of his obvious arousal pressed against her. Her lips trembled, and he kissed them, first tenderly, then hungrily, as if he could never get enough.

He yanked down the purple comforter, picked her up, and laid her gently on the sheets.

Then he climbed in bed with her and they made love to the chirping of the birds, beneath the rustle of the maples and oaks.

Poppy stretched her limbs until her hands and feet extended beyond the mattress and she sucked in a lungful of fresh country air, then relaxed completely, one arm slung over her head.

Above her was a canopy of scallop-edged leaves; surrounding her, birdsong.

And next to her lay her Heath.

"Did you know that ninety percent of our bodies is stardust?" he asked.

She laughed, feeling her stomach going up and down. "That's random. Especially since it's daytime."

"But the stars are still there, even if we can't see them."

He propped himself up on one elbow, picked up a lock of her hair, and tickled her chin with it.

She turned her head and looked up into his hazel eyes.

He kissed the tip of her nose.

She looked up through the leaves at snatches of azure and white. "Do you know what time it is?"

Heath frowned. "Why?"

"There's something I have to do."

He leaned over, picked up his jeans, and turned them around until he found the back pocket. "Twelve thirty-five."

She swung her legs over the side of the mattress.

"Where are you going?"

"To stop the sale of my café. The closing's at one."

Heath brightened. "You are the smartest, bravest person I know. Just one thing before you go."

She stopped from where she was gathering up her clothes and raised a questioning brow.

"If you're going to be sharing my bed from now on, does that mean I get my stuffed dog back?"

Chapter Thirty-three

A month after she'd moved into Heath's house, Poppy went over to give Kyle and Sandy Houser their lunch check. Next to them in an infant chair, their newborn son, Hawthorne, blew raspberries.

Sandy's four-year-old thrust a picture of a princess at Poppy.

"Here."

"For me?"

She nodded somberly.

"Who is this?"

She pointed to Poppy. "You."

"Me?" Her hand flew to her breast. "Why, thank you so much!"

"It's for your new picture wall."

"I will go right over and hang it up," said Poppy.

She did just that, hanging the child's drawing next to the eight-by-ten of her ad for Palette Cosmetics.

Poppy stood back with her hands on her hips to appraise the new second row of photos that she'd devised.

Demi Barnes, fists clenched in the pocket of her waitress uniform, came up to Poppy.

"Keval is insisting on hazelnut syrup in his Hairbender and we're out. What should I do?"

Poppy glanced over at where Keval held Miss Sweetie, hand-feeding her the toast he'd ordered while Poppy's chocolate Lab sat patiently, waiting for his dole. "None for Jackson," she called out. "He's getting to be a beast since I've been bringing him in here."

To Demi she lowered her voice and said, "Convince Keval that the caramel's equally good. And put hazelnut on the shopping list you're writing up for me."

Her mom came in wearing a sun visor and wraparound sunglasses. "Now, don't forget to clean the vent hoods and the ice machine next week. The HVAC guy is coming Tuesday. And—"

"I've got it, Mom. You just go now and have fun."

"Don't worry, we'll keep an eye on her," called Liz Greenburn from the table where she sat with Heath's dad, who was munching a muffin.

"Scarlett?" Big Pop entered wearing his fancy new driving cap, in search of his wife. Outside along the curb, their motor home idled loudly. "We're burning daylight. Poppy'll be fine. You can call her every day from the road."

"I know . . ." Mom gave Poppy a wistful look.

Poppy gave her a hug. "You heard him. Get going. I love you."

"Oh, I love you, too, honey. Take care."

"What is Demi doing working for Poppy?" asked Sam at the corner booth he shared with Red.

Red raised an eyebrow. "Government budget cutbacks are a bitch," she replied, smirking around the straw she held to her lips.

They watched Heath stroll in after pumping his future father-in-law's hand one last time before the Springers left on their extended trip south.

"Second question," said Sam as Heath greeted Poppy with a hug and a kiss. "What technique did you use to convince Poppy that Heath was the one?"

"Nothing but a little reverse psychology. How about you? How'd you light a fire under Heath?"

Sam laid his napkin beside his empty plate. "Chemists always have solutions."

To his satisfaction, Red groaned and rolled her eyes.

"Owens, you are so lame."

Sam folded his arms and leaned in. "Heath always knew what he had to do. All he needed was a shove in the right direction."

At that, she gave him a grin. "Up high," she said, raising her hand.

Their palms met with a resounding slap.

Acknowledgments

Intoxicating marks a turning point in my writing career. Kensington has announced that my next series, A Ribbon Ridge Romance, will be published in mass-market paperback as well as digitally. And it's all due to you, loyal readers. I can't thank you enough!

For me, novel writing is not so much about finding the right words as it is editing out the wrong ones. Getting to the heart of the story in much the same way that a sculptor carves away stone to reveal the statue underneath.

After months of hard labor, with the trepidation of a mother surrendering her newborn, the manuscript is finally delivered to its editor. I've been blessed to find a nurturing foster mother in my editor, Esi Sogah. With a few well-chosen words of her own, Esi zeroes in on just what is needed to make my books the best they can be.

Thank you to Esi, production editor Rebecca Cremonese, and *all* the professionals at Kensington Publishing who have helped nurture *Intoxicating*, our sixth book-baby.

Last, I want to mention how much fun I had researching real senior superlatives on the Web. I pored over dozens of clever examples in my quest to compose one that was uniquely Poppy. Thanks to all you bright young journalists for the inspiration. Keep writing. And never stop reading.

All the best,
Heather

Want more of the wine lovers of the Willamette Valley?
Keep an eye out for the next book in the series
And be sure to read
THE CRUSH
Available now from
Heather Heyford
And
Lyrical Shine

Heather Heyford learned to walk and talk in Texas, then moved to England. *("Y'all want some scones?")* While in Europe, Heather was forced by her cruel parents to spend Saturdays in the leopard vinyl back seat of their Peugeot, motoring from one medieval pile to the next for the lame purpose of "learning something." What she soon learned was how to allay the boredom by stashing a *Cosmo* under the seat. Now a recovering teacher, Heather writes romance novels set in the wine country. She is represented by the Nancy Yost Literary Agency.

A PERFECT PAIRING

Juniper Hart has her dream job—or rather, her dream job has her. Under Junie's management, the winery her late father started is finally getting noticed. But she's lonely, deep in debt, and overwhelmed with work. Even if she had time to date, the only men she meets are smug, stemware-breaking hotshots like Lieutenant Manolo Santos, whose good looks and smooth charm don't half make up for the sour taste he leaves on Junie's palate.

After years as an army engineer and a childhood in a restaurant kitchen, Manolo can see Junie's winery is about to go sideways— and he's bursting with ideas to help. Except Junie's far too magnetic for comfort. He left New Jersey to escape becoming one more Santos man shackled to a captivating woman and a failing family business. But in the misty hills of Oregon, with a sip of supple pinot on his tongue, pulling away is the last thing he wants to do . . .

HEATHER
HEYFORD
The Crush

AN OREGON WINE COUNTRY ROMANCE

shine

A TASTE OF CHARDONNAY

Join author Heather Heyford as she uncorks a sparkling new series following the St. Pierre sisters, heiresses to a Napa wine fortune who are toasting the good life and are thirsty for love . . .

Chardonnay St. Pierre's father is as infamous for his scandals as he is famous for his wine, and it's up to Char to restore the family name. The Challenge, an elite charity competition held in Napa, seems like the perfect opportunity for the socialite to cement her image as a philanthropist. But all eyes—including Char's—are on the Hollywood heartthrob who's also entered the race . . .

Long before his face was splashed across the gossip magazines, Ryder McBride grew up in a working-class family in Napa. He knows all about the St. Pierre sisters and their notorious father, and when he learns he'll be up against Char in The Challenge, he assumes the grape doesn't fall far from the vine. But the more they get to know one another, the more they begin to realize that nothing pairs better with a heated rivalry than a healthy pour of flirtation . . .

HEATHER HEYFORD

A Taste of Chardonnay

THE NAPA WINE HEIRESSES

A TASTE OF MERLOT

Raise your glass and join Heather Heyford as she pours a second serving in her series following these headstrong wine heiresses in their quest to strike out on their own . . .

Merlot St. Pierre is struggling to break free from her family name. Her college classmates whisper behind her back that her passion for jewelry design is little more than a hobby, since she'll always have her father's fortune. But Meri is determined to prove them wrong, and with the help of a handsome jewelry buyer, she just may taste her first sip of success—as long as she can hide who she really is . . .

Mark Newman's family owns a chain of high-end jewelry stores, and he's working hard to get out from under his aunt's thumb and prove he has a good eye *and* a head for business. He's certain Meri's designs could be the next big thing, but he'll have to convince her that she can use her famous last name to her advantage. As their business partnership takes root, an attraction begins to flourish—but they'll both find that love, like wine, takes time to perfect . . .

HEATHER HEYFORD
A Taste of Merlot

THE NAPA WINE HEIRESSES

A TASTE OF SAUVIGNON

Join Heather Heyford as she returns to Napa for a third taste in her series following three wine heiresses, each as vibrant and unique as the grapes for which they were named . . .

Sauvignon St. Pierre has always been fiercely ambitious. She easily could've cashed in on her family's fortune, but instead she struck out on her own, breezed through law school, and landed a job at a small firm in Napa. Savvy's life is as tidy and straightforward as her sizable collection of little black dresses, and she likes it that way—but every now and then, she can't help but long for her first sip of love . . .

After a chance encounter with Esteban Morales, the *caliente* son of Papa St. Pierre's long-time rival, something inside Savvy wakes up. It could be that Esteban's interest in cultivating lavender appeals to her passion for perfumery. But there's something else about the charming but down-to-earth farmer that she simply can't resist. They both know their families are an unlikely pairing, but together, Savvy and Esteban just may be the ideal varietals for a perfect blend . . .

HEATHER HEYFORD

A Taste of Sauvignon

shine
LYRICAL

THE NAPA WINE HEIRESSES

A TASTE OF SAKE

As author Heather Heyford pours a final glass in her series following three Napa wine heiresses, a newcomer must work her way into a tightly-knit family whose bond has been fermenting for years . . .

Though they each have their own ambitions and are known to be competitive—even with one another—the St. Pierre sisters are fiercely loyal. Chardonnay and Merlot are thrilled about Sauvignon's wedding day, and it's slated to be the soirée of the decade among Napa's most elite residents. Given the family's notoriety, it almost stands to reason that their eccentric father, Xavier, would arrive by helicopter. But no one could have anticipated the wedding surprise he'd brought along with him . . .

The product of one of Xavier's many affairs, Sake is introduced as the half-Japanese sister the St. Pierre girls never knew they had. She struggles to break into clique-ish Napa society—and getting in with her sisters is proving more difficult than nabbing a '74 Cabernet. It seems only high-end realtor Bill Diamond can tell there's more to Sake than meets the eye. Afraid of repeating her mother's mistakes, Sake just hopes that getting drunk on love won't leave her with a hangover of rejection . . .

HEATHER HEYFORD

A Taste of Sake

THE NAPA WINE HEIRESSES

CPSIA information can be obtained
at www.ICGtesting.com
Printed in the USA
LVOW11s1638130317
527031LV00001B/242/P